I0618131

OUT

OF

HAND

By

Kathy L. Salt

2017

Out of Hand © 2017 Kathy L. Salt
Triplicity Publishing, LLC

ISBN-13: 978-0999737019
ISBN-10: 0999737015

This is a work of fiction. Names, characters, places, and incidents are the product of the author's imagination and are used fictitiously. Any resemblance to actual persons, living or dead, business establishments, events of any kind, or locales is entirely coincidental.
Printed in the United States of America

First Edition – 2017
Cover Design: Triplicity Publishing, LLC
Interior Design: Triplicity Publishing, LLC
Editor: Haley White - Triplicity Publishing, LLC

Acknowledgement

A big thank you to Marco, Teresa, Kim and Deniz, who have commented, criticized and helped me along the way. A thank you to my little sister who is always ready to laugh or cry with me. I would also like to thank my editor Haley White who made editing my story seem easy. Last I want to thank my parents who, no matter how cliché it sounds, have always believed in me.

Dedication

To Lud-
who has my heart, no kidnapping necessary.

Chapter One

A bell rang inside the store and made Mimi look up from her sewing machine. She brushed a few stray threads from her clothes and got up, the half-finished dress on her lap falling to the floor. She was in the staff room—or what would have been her staff room if she had any regular staff. It was late in the afternoon, just fifteen minutes before closing and there hadn't been any customers for over an hour.

She was about to head into the store when there was a knocking on the door.

"I'm coming!" she called. She had a pretty good idea who it was, but it felt better to go to into the store rather than just invite them in. She couldn't count out the possibility that it was a customer out for a late shopping spree.

She opened the door and smiled at her best friend Paige. She was standing next to the register with a bottle of wine in her hand.

"Hey there." Mimi glanced at clock on the wall. "At least you waited until closing hours this time." She went to lock the door of the store. "Well, close enough."

"The kids at work drove me crazy," Paige groaned. "Why did you let me become a kindergarten teacher? I hate children."

Mimi chuckled.

"I don't remember having any say in the matter."

1

Paige made a face and stuck her tongue out.

"Just drink with me, okay?" she said. "You know that if you don't need a drink on Friday you didn't work hard enough during the week."

"I've heard that mantra before."

Paige turned off the light in the shop. She looked over the now dark dresses and skirts and trousers that hung there. The clothes contained her blood, sweat, and pierced fingertips. *I really need to hire someone to help me with the sewing.* And it just wasn't profitable to hand sew all your own merchandise. Not when you were trying to make it as a seamstress in the middle of London. Whenever the thought came to mind, Mimi felt overwhelmed. She shook her head, trying to clear her mind. It was Friday. She didn't want to think about work anymore.

She followed Paige into the staff room. The place where she spent the day sewing when there were no customers in the store. She did have one employee, who worked all Wednesdays, Fridays, and Saturdays. But Mimi was ultimately in charge of the designing and making of her clothes. It was an understatement to say that Mimi worked twenty-four hours a day.

Luckily this wasn't the first time Paige showed up at the end of day, and she knew that Mimi kept glasses for little get-togethers just like this one. She prepared their drinks while Mimi cleared the table of fabrics. Paige also pulled a chair from the corner and sat down on it.

The second-hand chair that was no doubt twenty years old creaked loudly when Mimi finally sank down on it. She kicked off her pumps and put her feet up Paige's knees. Paige tweaked her big toe.

"Your back hurting?" Paige, God bless her, didn't even ask her to remove her feet.

"Always." Sitting over the sewing machine for sometimes hours on end really did take it out on her back. She welcomed the evening with open arms. She'd rather focus on Paige's continuous chatter anyways and forget about the bills she was hiding on top of the closet.

"... and then he held the shovel aimed at my face. Of course I was calm on the outside, but on the inside I was sure that I was going to die."

Mimi tried to smile and pretend like she wasn't worrying about her imminent financial doom and failure.

"Sounds difficult." She took another sip of her drink.

"The little shits, I tell you." Paige finished off her first glass and right away poured herself a second one. Mimi was still working on her first.

"We're still going out tonight, right? After dinner of course." Paige looked at her.

Mimi bit her lip.

"I don't know. No money."

"Awww." Paige put her glass down and reached across the table. She sloppily patted Mimi's black hair. "Poor Mimi. It'll be my treat, okay? I just need to dance my troubles away and I'm not doing it alone. You'll force me to call my sister, and you don't want me to do that, do you?" She made a face.

Mimi smiled and in one go finished her glass.

"You win, we can go."

*

As thrilling as it was to pass by airport security carrying an illegal package, there was nothing quite like sinking into a bath after a long day. Leo could calm the fluttering butterflies in her stomach and revel in the fact that she had once more gotten away with a crime.

After taking her time in the tub—after all she deserved it—Leo stood up, the water falling down the length of her body. She rinsed off any remnants of soap or shampoo, and reached for a towel. After drying off most of the excess water, she toweled her hair as she walked into the bedroom.

She opened up her trusted and worn leather duffel bag and pulled out a pair of black jeans and a white button-down shirt. Once dressed, she returned to the bathroom to brush her dark hair until it shone like a waterfall down her shoulders. She smiled at herself in the mirror. *Yeah, that will do.*

Leo wasn't intending to take another job for a few days now. Even smugglers needed vacation after all. And London was definitely better than the small village in the middle of nowhere Leo had spent the last couple of days in. It wasn't a place to be bored in. Leo hated being bored.

Her stomach rumbled and she patted it with a grimace. As usual, she had forgotten about food. *Fine, dinner.* But first she needed to take care of a couple of things.

She got her leather bag from the bedroom and reached for an envelope, a small box, and some carbon paper. Carbon paper was perfect for concealing money or papers from airport security. It worked so well that even an x-ray couldn't pick up on it most of the time. She brought it all to the living room and put it on the sofa table, but not before grabbing two books from the book case.

She opened the envelope. She usually didn't care about what currency she was paid in, all she had to do was wait until the exchange rate was in her favor, but it helped when the client had paid her in *one* currency and not four different kinds. She flipped through the notes. *No. Five different currencies.* Leo sighed as she found two Brazilian *real* notes too. *I should tell Sandra to not accept another job from Mr. Martin.* She reached for her bag again and took out a notepad and a pen. She could use the calculator on her phone.

Sixty-five percent of the money belonged to Sandra Sousa, her boss, and after calculating the right amount, Leo set those aside first. She worked her fingers carefully, folding the carbon around the bills and placed them in the box between two books. She taped the box shut and wrote an address for a post box in Portugal.

When the box was ready, Leo counted her own money again. She knew how much it was from before, but she liked the feeling of money in her hands. It was less than usual, but enough for now. What she held in her hand was food and maybe some new socks. She had no saving plan, no bank account, no real home. What she had in her hand was it. The simple papers in her hand was her *life*.

She put most of the money back inside the envelope, and put the envelope in a special compartment inside her bag. The rest she put in her wallet. It was dinner time.

*

After a perfect meal of noodles and every vegetable under the sun, Leo roamed around Soho looking for somewhere to waste time. The idea of dancing close to a female body, moving to a deafening beat and then falling into bed together was more than motivating. It was with that goal Leo chose between the clubs that existed in this infamous part of London. She eventually chose one at random. "The All-Nighter" the yellow and green flashing neon sign said, and Leo hoped it would hold up to that promise.

She danced for a bit, but stopped quite soon. It was a straight bar, and the music just wasn't to her taste. *I should have gone to an LGBT one.* It wasn't the first time she had made this mistake.

Hoping that alcohol would make the music sound better, she sat down in front of the bar and ordered a beer. As sparsely populated as the dance floor had been, Leo had to fight her way to the bar. She finally managed to wedge herself in between an old man drinking alone and two women who were discussing something in loud voices.

At first Leo didn't mind their chatter, she just lifted her hand and ordered a beer. While she waited, she gazed at the colorful bottles that sat behind the bartender. In the flashing lights of the bar, they seemed to shine, reminding her of — a bony elbow was jabbed into her ribs, hard.

"Ouch!" Leo turned to face the loud women to her right. "Do you mind?"

Two dark brown, nearly black, eyes focused on her.

"I'm sorry." But the woman's smile was wide and her gaze a little unfocused, like she was drowning but liking it.

Leo rolled her eyes and didn't reply. The bartender handed her a beer and she grabbed it, took a quick sip. The music wasn't good yet.

"Fuck," the other woman exclaimed, the one who hadn't hit Leo. Her voice was so loud that Leo didn't have any choice but to hear. "Damn, Jonas has broken his arm."

"I thought he was with his dad this weekend. Come on, don't leave me here."

"He broke his arm, Mimi, I need to go. I'll text you tomorrow, okay?"

"Don't leave me," the girl said, but her friend didn't listen as she ran off. Leaving Mimi alone by the bar, next to Leo.

"I should have stayed at home," she muttered. Then she made a gesture to the bartender. "A gin and tonic, please." She took out a wallet from inside her purse, opened the zipper, and turned it upside down. A myriad of coins poured out and she started counting them, most of them the bright copper-tint of pennies. Leo glanced at her.

Mimi shrugged apologetically at the bartender who scraped the money off of the bar with a wistful smile and placed the drink in front of her.

While Mimi started nursing on her drink, Leo ordered another beer. The music had gotten increasingly better. More nuances and less cheap Eurobeat.

"I hate this club," Mimi said out loud after a little while. "I should never have let Paige convince me to go out tonight."

Leo wasn't sure if Mimi was just voicing her thoughts or actually talking to her, so she stayed quiet and focused on the tall beer glass in front. Occasionally, she couldn't help but glance to the side. As aggravating as Mimi was, Leo had to admit that she was pretty. Spitfire eyes, shapely lips covered with a red lipstick that contrasted her pale skin and black hair nicely. She was Southeast Asian, but her accent was something else. A strangely neutral mix between European and American.

"What about you?" Mimi looked at her. "Are you from around here?" There was a sharpness to her voice, more accusing than making friendly conversation.

"No." Not wanting to talk anymore, Leo got up from the bar. She wanted to dance.

"Where are you from then?" Mimi spun around, stretched her hand out and toppled over. Before Leo even had fully assessed what was happening, she, purely out of instinct, caught the young woman in her arms. *Great, a young girl who doesn't know how much alcohol she can take.*

"How many drinks have you had?" She pushed Mimi fully upright but kept her grip on her arm. As annoying as Mimi was, she kept swaying back and forth, and Leo didn't want to just let her fall.

"None." Mimi's speech was slightly slurred. "That was my first. Well I had some wine earlier but that was hours ago." She looked at Leo, her eyes wide and unfocused. She looked more than drunk. She looked high.

Leo put both hands on her shoulders and shook her.

"Are you sure?" She shook her again. "Mimi, this is important. You haven't drunk anything heavier?"

"You can't call me Mimi. I don't know you." She looked indignant but then whimpered and put a hand to her stomach. "I feel sick."

Leo swore under her breath. Her instincts kicked in and she scanned the club for anything suspicious. Who would have tried to drug a girl drinking with her friend? Then again, her friend had left.

Leo looked at the barkeep. He could have—

Mimi groaned and grabbed her arm with both hands. Leo looked at her. What was she going to do now? Whether roofie or medical condition, something was clearly wrong with Mimi. And for some reason, she was now clinging on Leo's arm. *Great, I'm now stuck babysitting a girl who can't even hold an eye on her drink, there goes my night off.* Leo might have been a crook, but she wasn't going to just leave a young woman in trouble.

8

Maybe I can just put her in a taxi, Leo thought as she led Mimi out of the club. It was colder out of the club, and she hoped that the refreshing breeze would sober the young woman up. There was a taxi right outside that Leo pushed Mimi into. As long as Mimi had enough presence to tell the taxi driver where to take her, Leo could simply—

"No!" Mimi reached out of the car and grabbed Leo's wrist, her grip weak. Her eyes were wide and for a millisecond focused on Leo. "Don't leave me. Please! I feel so weird..." She licked her lips, closed her eyes, and fell backwards across the seats.

Leo didn't hesitate, she just slid inside the car. She moved Mimi's legs so that she had enough room to sit down. She didn't look at Mimi, instead closed the door and crossed her arms. *That's it, night ruined.*

"Where to?" the driver asked.

"One moment." Leo turned to Mimi and gently tapped her cheek. "Where do you live?"

Mimi mumbled something and Leo had to put her ear close to Mimi's mouth to make out her address. She referred the address to the driver and then settled down on her seat. She didn't react when Mimi got up and rested her head on her shoulder. Leo didn't think much about it, except that Mimi smelled only faintly of wine, which reinforced Leo's suspicions that she had been drugged. Rohypnol maybe. Or Ketamine. Leo hoped that it wasn't something too heavy.

Ten minutes later the car pulled to a halt and, with a groan, Leo handed a few hard earned notes to the driver, then she maneuvered herself and Mimi out of the car.

As the taxi drove away, Leo looked at the building in front of her with Mimi hanging off of her shoulder.

"Can you walk?"

Out of Hand

Mimi nodded against her arm, but Leo didn't dare to let go of her. Together they staggered toward the doors on the apartment complex. When they had reached the one closest to them, Mimi spoke up.

"4-A." Her voice was small and full of sleep. None of the former edge was there.

"Right-ie then." Leo walked toward the door that said 4-A in big grey letters. "Do you have any keys?"

"Purse." Somehow Mimi's purse had stayed there, hanging around her neck. *Huh, I wonder when that got there.* It was lucky, because Leo would never have thought of checking for it before this.

She grabbed it with her free hand, and with minimal effort got the clasp open with the one hand. She took the keyring out. It held several keys. Leo stared at them for less than a minute but before she could start trying them, Mimi reached out and pointed at the longest one.

*

As soon as Leo turned on the light switch she did a double take. Fabrics of different kinds were lying everywhere, strewn across the sofa, in piles on the table and floors. In the middle of the room, in front of a kitchenette, a large sewing machine stood proudly, as if on the honorary place on the table. Clearly Mimi made clothes, either professionally or passionately. Most likely both, Leo thought.

Mimi made a snoring noise and leaned even heavier against Leo's side. She was asleep. Before she fell, Leo lifted her up, she was a slight thing after all, and carried her toward the bed in the other corner. Apart from two small doors, leading to bathroom and closet, Leo guessed, Mimi's apartment only had one door.

"I'm going to get you a bucket and a glass of water, okay?" Leo placed her on the bed, Mimi's body limp like a doll's. "You're going to need it."

She tiptoed to the kitchenette and looked through the cabinet over the sink for glasses; she grabbed a large one and poured water in it. She also found a trash can under the sink and brought both to Mimi's bedside.

"Here you go," she said as she placed them by the bed. Mimi didn't say anything or even react to Leo's voice, just breathed deeply.

Leo looked at her for a moment and then rolled her over so that she was on her stomach with her face on the side. *Just in case she throws up.*

Done with playing nursemaid for the night, Leo left. But not before locking and then pulling the door closed. Satisfied with her actions, she headed home.

*

When the buzzing of her phone woke her up, Leo didn't reach for it at first. She had been in the middle of a dream and was in no way ready to wake up. It was still too early. Eventually, Leo groaned and reached for it; she looked at the screen. It was Sandra. Leo wrinkled her eyebrows, sleepiness leaving her fast. Sandra never called her anymore.

"Can you explain something to me?" Sandra didn't wait for Leo to say anything before she started talking, her usual smooth voice sharp. For Leo it was almost possible to hear the way her mouth curled in annoyance.

"What?" Leo couldn't help the grogginess in her voice, she sat up and pulled her fingers through her hair.

"I just had a call from Mila, asking me why I sent two of you to do a one-person job."

11

Mila was another courier, but Leo had only met her once or twice before. Office parties weren't common in their line of work.

"A job?" Leo scratched her head with her free hand. "What job? I don't have a job right now."

"Really?" Sandra sounded disbelieving. "Because according to Mila you escorted a woman home last night."

What? Leo rubbed her eyes with her knuckles. *Was she still dreaming?* She turned on the light by her side, trying to wake up. Maybe she had heard wrong. She had done nothing yesterday, nothing at… *Oh.* The memories of last night came back. Mimi. The supposed drugs.

"There was a woman. She was in trouble," Leo mumbled. "Seemed drugged. I couldn't let her get hurt or—"

"Or lost," Sandra hissed. "Which is exactly what was supposed to happen. Mila had been hired to extract Kazumi Adam and bring her to Hal's tonight. Instead you stepped in and apparently played white knight and took her home!"

"What?" Leo couldn't believe what she was hearing, "Extract? No, wait! That makes no sense. I helped a woman named Mimi home, she was with a friend. I didn't see Mila anywhere, I—" She fell silent. Had Mila been there? Leo didn't really know her and maybe in her own buzzed state there was a possibility that Leo had missed her.

"Mila operates covertly, you know this. You weren't supposed to see her."

"I'm sorry." Leo laid back down, placing her arm with the back of her hand against her eyes. *Gosh, I fucked up. What is Sandra thinking?*

"You need to fix this, Leonora."

Leo's heart sank. As much as she wanted to say "yes, anything," she didn't like the tone of Sandra's voice.

"What do you need me to do?"

"The obvious," Sandra replied. "Mila is offended and is refusing to finish the job. You need to move Kazumi to Hal's. I'll be in touch once that's done." Sandra hung up. She hadn't even waited to hear if Leo agreed.

What the fuck just happened? Leo threw the phone on the mattress. Kidnapping was definitely not part of her job description, but she wasn't sure how much of a choice she had. She liked her life. She liked her job. She more than liked Sandra. She didn't want to do anything to jeopardize it. If Sandra asked her to jump, Leo asked how high, and if Sandra asked her to kidnap a young woman, Leo asked where to take her.

Chapter Two

Mimi's head was pounding and her mouth was so dry her tongue was sticking to the ceiling of her mouth. Her body felt like the bruised part of an apple, way too tender and way too soft. She felt wrong. Everything just hurt. She opened her eyes, not sure what she would see.

The first thing she saw was the outline of her bathroom door. Then she noticed the magazine-ladened nightstand, the familiar rug that she had had since she was little. She was *home*. She breathed in and out. Home. No matter what had happened earlier, the most important thing was that she had somehow found her way home.

She scrunched up her face, trying to remember. Paige had met her at the store, hadn't she? Like usual. They had gone out —? *Paige!* She had to call Paige! Wasn't her child hurt?

Mimi flew up from the bed only to fall back down on her pillow, clutching her head. The room didn't stay still, it went around, around, around and she turned to her side, over the edge of the bed. Luckily there was a trashcan there and she didn't have to throw up on the floor.

When she was done she pulled back, disgusted with herself. Was she ill? Did she have a hangover? But she didn't drink much, she never did. Maybe she really was ill and the alcohol had just made it much worse. That had to be it.

The spinning room had come to a somewhat halt and Mimi gratefully reached out for the glass of water that stood on top of her pile of fashion magazines on the bedside table. The glass was room temperature but still wonderfully cool in her dry mouth. She put it back and then kept her gaze on it. A glass of water. The trashcan. Who had fixed those things? Had she herself? Or someone else? Mimi held still. There was a car alarm somewhere outside, and the buzzing of her fridge seemed louder than usual, but otherwise there were no sounds out of the ordinary.

She rolled out of bed with a groan and went to search for her phone. Her purse was standing on a pile of fabrics near the front door. Both her phone and wallet were there. She cradled her phone in her hand, and called Paige.

The signals were too loud for Mimi's tired head, and she prayed for Paige to answer soon so they would stop.

"Mimi! Hey!"

Mimi changed her mind. Paige's alto voice was just as bad as the signals.

"Paige." Hearing the familiar voice made Mimi feel worse. At once, she lost all that she wanted to say.

"Gosh, you sound terrible. What happened after I left last night?"

Mimi swallowed back sudden tears, and she closed her fist so hard her pink and sparkling nails dug into her palm.

"I must have gotten very drunk." She tried to sound normal. "I'm not sure. But I'm home in one piece, on my own, and my purse is with me."

"Oh, honey. I'm so sorry, are you okay? Did someone take care of you?"

"Yes." Mimi closed her eyes, trying hard to remember. "There must have been." Her head pounded. "Listen, I think I need to take a shower." Her voice sounded croaky and her throat felt as if it was lined with sandpaper.

"Gosh, you sound really bad." Paige tone was soft. "Go and rest okay? We'll talk later."

"Mmm." Mimi could only make an affirmative noise as her mouth filled with saliva. "Bye."

Without waiting for an answer, she turned off the call, threw the phone on the bed, and ran to the bathroom to throw up again.

*

Mimi had hoped to feel better after a shower; after brushing the night from her mouth and drinking a big glass of water, but her state remained unchanged. The idea of roofies and other drugs went through her head, but surely she wouldn't have been home if she had been drugged and…. She couldn't finish the sentence, even inside the safety of her own head. No, she decided, it was just a bad reaction to alcohol, maybe mixed with a head cold. There were no signs of any bumps or bruises. Or scratches. Apart from the strange feeling in her head and chest, she seemed fine.

She patted her body with one of her cheap, coarse towels, grimacing when it ripped at her skin. Dry and naked, she went over to the wardrobe that stood next to her bed.

She picked a pale blue blouse and a grey maxi skirt with a leather belt from her closet. Both were her creations and she felt proud putting them on. She did her best to ignore the nagging guilt that it was better for her to sell them. But she still needed to wear clothes. And it was cheaper to wear clothes she had made herself than go shopping.

She slid low wedge shoes on her feet and grabbed her purse. She was still nauseated and her head was spinning a little bit, but it wasn't going to stop her from getting through the business of the day. Her beckoning bills didn't allow her the privilege of taking a day off. It was Sunday, and her store was closed, but that meant she could go through her inventory and maybe even do some sewing if she took her sewing machine with her.

After stumbling twice when trying to get the things she needed, she had to stop and take off the wedges. As pretty as her shoes were, she couldn't wear them this morning. It just didn't work. She didn't want to wear her running shoes. After all, they clashed with the rest of her outfit, but she also didn't have much choice. She didn't want to fall on her face outside just because she was vain. Well, not first thing in the morning anyway.

Once in more sensible shoes, she got a box of fabric and also packaged her sewing machine. It was an older model, the plastic burnt on the side, that she had gotten second hand when she had moved to London to open her shop. She had her eyes on a newer model, but didn't think she would ever fully retire this one. It meant too much.

She also grabbed her purse from the kitchen table and went outside, kicking the door closed in the process.

She took a few steps down the stairs but had to stop, her head spun and she feared she would topple over. *What's wrong with me? Maybe I should go to the doctor?* She tried to breathe calmly, but it only helped minimally as waves of wanting to throw up again washed over her.

As she exited the building she started wondering if it would be safe for her to drive at all. She shook her head, determined to give it a go. She couldn't afford to take a sick-day. Not this early in the financial year. *If I still feel bad tomorrow, maybe I could ask*—Mimi's train of thought stopped as she turned around the corner and walked right into another person, making her drop all her boxes. She groaned at the hard *clonk* the box containing her precious sewing machine made when it hit the ground.

"I'm sorry," the other woman said, but Mimi couldn't answer at first. She just stared at her boxes, feeling anger rise in her chest.

She looked up and took a step back. She knew the other woman from somewhere. There was something familiar about her long dark hair, gangly frame, and thin mouth. She was wearing shades but took them off, revealing thoughtful blue eyes. Where had Mimi seen her before?

Not from my shop, she thought with a leer while taking in the woman's faded black jeans, leather jacket, and white T-shirt. No, definitely not hers. Too mainstream, too regular, too—Mimi panicked when the world started spinning again, even worse this time. Not having any choice, she grabbed the woman's arm, not wanting to fall face-first on the sidewalk.

"Hey! You okay?" Muscles flexed under Mimi's fingers and a hand came to rest on her back. There was something familiar about this too.

"Do I look okay?" She hated the feeling of not being in control of her own body. She clung to the woman's arm like she was drowning and felt secretly relieved when a helping arm was placed around her shoulders.

"Do you remember me?"

The question first caught Mimi off guard, but guessing wasn't difficult. She still couldn't remember where she had seen her; there was only one real guess she could make.

"From last night?" She wanted to look up and take another glance, but the sudden vertigo didn't allow her. *Don't throw up, don't throw up, don't throw up.*

"Yes." The woman's accent was funny. German.

Mimi sucked in breath through her teeth and swallowed against another wave of nausea.

"What happened last night?"

"I'm not sure." She sounded unsure. Guilty. "I think someone slipped something in your drink. I helped you home."

"Did we…?" *If she took advantage of me, she's going to get my sewing machine in her head. I don't care if it breaks.* Mimi forced herself to raise her head and lock eyes with her nighttime savior.

"Of course not." The woman shook her head. "I'm Leo, by the way. I don't think you remember my name from last night." She smiled, but the smile didn't quite reach her eyes. She put the sunglasses on again.

"Mimi." Mimi could have given her real name, but her nickname sounded better. This Leo had seen her at her worse. Mimi didn't want to give her the intimacy of knowing her full name as well. "Thank you, Leo, for taking care of me last night. I remember I was with a friend, but—"

"She left early."

"That she did." Mimi exhaled, praying to stay upright. "Well. Thanks again."

She bent down to pick up her boxes but stopped halfway. An embarrassing whimper escaped her as she put a hand to her forehead. The world really needed to stay still for a while so she could do her job.

"Where are you going with all these fabrics? To work?" Surprise filled Leo's voice. "Are you sure that's wise?"

"I have to." Mimi really did have to, but no matter how much she wanted she couldn't will herself to lean down even further and grab her sewing machine. She didn't even stop to wonder how Leo knew what she did for living. *Oh yeah, she saw my place last night, right?*

"Let me help you." Leo picked up the boxes before Mimi had even replied.

"Don't be silly," she said. "Of course you don't have to help me." She tried to ignore how it was hard to stand up without Leo's support. She swayed from side to side. *Damn it, what do I do now?*

"Are you driving?"

Mimi was trying to pull the box with her sewing machine from Leo's grip.

"Yes." She couldn't keep the irritation from her voice. "I don't have much choice, okay? Thank you for taking care of me last night, but right now I really need to go."

Leo's eyes were wide as she handed both boxes to her. Mimi struggled under the weight. Had her sewing machine always been this heavy? When she lifted her gaze, Leo was silently watching her.

"Let me drive you."

Mimi raised one of her eyebrows.

"You want to drive me?"

"Please." Leo nodded. "I'd hate for my efforts last night to go to waste if you get hurt today in an accident."

Mimi didn't want to accept it, but she had to admit that it was the wiser choice. The nausea had settled for the moment, but it had been replaced by a throbbing headache and she knew that she couldn't be legally trusted behind the wheel. Leo had offered after all. Mimi had to admit that all she wanted to do was lay down on the ground and die.

"If you don't mind terribly." *Fine.* "I'd be grateful."

Leo looked relieved. *No, I must be mistaken, why would she be relieved?* Mimi didn't think any more of it as Leo relieved her of one of the boxes, and then let Mimi lead her to the car.

As strange as it was being helped by a stranger, Mimi did feel immensely grateful when all she had to do was sink down on the passenger seat with a sigh. She dug for a water bottle in her purse and drank from it in big, greedy gulps.

Leo sat down in the driver's seat and didn't look at Mimi as she started the car.

"The address is—" Mimi started, but Leo interrupted her.

"I don't need it." Leo's voice was empty.

"What do you mean you don't need it? Of course you need it. I need to go to my shop. That's where you're taking me." Mimi tried to sit up straighter, but the fear that trickled down her spine brought the nausea back. She swallowed.

"No, I'm not." Leo put the car in a higher gear as she pulled out on the street. She pressed on a key and all the doors in the car locked.

Mimi looked at her with an open mouth. She wanted to process what was happening, but her mind refused to work. She wanted to complain, fight. Try to overtake Leo and fight for the wheel. Maybe knock her out with a punch. But she did nothing, her body was frozen.

Out of Hand

Her head spun as she stared in shock and disbelief as Leo drove herself, Mimi, the sewing machine, and Mimi's little car out of London.

Chapter Three

Leo had never been a planner. Which was an odd thing considering that in her line of work even the tiniest mistake could be the end of the operation. Most smugglers probably had a brilliant masterplan for each job. And a Plan B in case something went wrong. And a Plan C just to be sure. But Leo never did. Making so many plans that she could lose herself in them wasn't her thing. She didn't plan. She *reacted*. Leo didn't need a plan, she had her instincts. Her talent for improvisation had saved her more than once.

But kidnapping an adult person required a different kind of praxis. To kidnap someone, you needed a plan. Leo should have known all of that and still had headed to Mimi's place without one. All she had known was that she would go to Mimi's place, find her very hungover and in bed, and then... well, she would have decided when she got there.

What she hadn't anticipated was an obvious workaholic heading to work while hardly able to walk. *Idiot.* But so very, very good for Leo. It had been too easy. She couldn't believe that she was actually out of London with her 'package.'

Mimi had been completely quiet during the whole ride so far, and when Leo stole a glance at her she could see that she was very pale. Her complexion had taken on a green tone. *She better not throw up.*

"What the fuck is wrong with you?" Mimi hissed when their gazes met. "Are you some big creepy kidnapper?"

Her voice had a hard edge to it, as if she was more pissed off than scared, and against her better judgment, Leo was impressed. She didn't answer and turned her gaze back to the wheel. She guessed she should have been more concerned over what to do next, but she kept cruising along the road, not even breaching the speed limit. It was better to act normal than call the attention of the police.

She had to stop somewhere of course. Call Sandra. Hal too. And book tickets for the ferry from Dover to Calais. *Hmm. I need to figure out the ferry situation.* Leo stole another glance at her little prisoner.

"I need to throw up." Mimi sucked in air through her mouth but instead of puffy cheeks, Mimi looked determined. Leo wasn't a fool. *She just wants you to stop the car so she can try to get away.*

"Use some of the fabrics in the back." It was a test, and from Mimi's stunned silence, Leo knew that she had won.

"That's my livelihood, you know," Mimi said. "Those fabrics weren't cheap."

The need to throw up seemed forgotten, and Leo ignored her.

"Are you stupid?" Venom dropped from every word that came out of Mimi's mouth when she continued to talk. "Were you dropped on your head as a child? I demand you stop the car and let me go right now."

"That's not happening."

Leo didn't care about Mimi, she could say anything, do anything, it wouldn't stop Leo from doing what had to be done. After all, Sandra was counting on her.

*

Mimi sank back into her seat and looked out of the window. The trees were still flying by. She was still feeling a bit queasy, but her head was pounding a little bit less and her mind was clear. Her only goal had to be to earn her freedom.

And then never drink again. Whether her drink had been spiked or not, her mother had been right, drinking never led to anything good and was definitely not becoming of young ladies. Apparently, it led to their kidnapping. Mimi snorted.

She turned to her side and observed her kidnapper. The idiot. The creep. The liar. It really was too bad that she was also so gorgeous. Strong, slender arms, a dangerous look in her eyes, and a hard line for a mouth. Mimi shook her head and looked away. She must be sicker than she thought to be thinking something like that in a time like this.

She glanced at her purse that lay abandoned by her feet. Maybe she could reach for her phone and call someone? Paige was the obvious answer. Mimi didn't think that her brother would take her serious, and she would rather let Leo steal her away than call her parents. No, the only one she could call was Paige.

Maybe the key to getting away was acting completely normal. She leaned down and reached for her phone inside the purse.

"What are you doing?" Leo asked without taking her eyes off of the road.

"I just want to call Paige and tell her I'm away on an excursion. As exciting as it is travelling with a handsome stranger, I can't let my friends worry." She had barely

25

finished her sentence when Leo's large hand came as if out of nowhere and took her phone from her hands.

Mimi could only stare while Leo opened the window and threw her phone out of it.

"That was a gift," she growled, furious with Leo. Inside her ribs, her heart fluttered with fear. Before, she could have almost believed that this was some sick practical joke, but Leo's actions proved otherwise. For the first time, real fear gripped at Mimi's insides.

"Oh, God. Oh, God. Oh, God. I have seen her face, she's going to have no choice but to kill me," she mumbled to herself.

"I'm not going to kill you." Leo's voice suggested that it was an absurd idea, but Mimi wasn't so sure.

"Steal my organs and sell them on the black market?" Panic was settling in the pit of Mimi's stomach, and she searched her mind for any other reasons that Leo might have kidnapped her. "Sell me as a slave to the highest bidder? Rape me?"

Mimi's last question seemed to punch Leo as she produced an angry sound somewhere between a snort and growl.

"Of course not," she snapped. "I'd never hurt anyone that way."

Mimi wasn't convinced but knew she needed to calm down. She looked out of the window instead, trying to focus on a single point, but it was hard. The trees were flying past too quickly outside, making her head spin again. She fell forward, cradling her head in her hands and whimpered.

"You're not dying on me, are you?" Leo said. "Come on, you think I'm that gullible?"

Mimi could only groan in reply. If Leo thought she was dying, maybe she would stop the car and Mimi could escape. She let her body go limp and fell forward. She stayed like that, hanging lifeless in her seat belt.

Leo swore and she snickered silently to herself. Even if she didn't manage to run away, making her kidnapper panic was worth the extra vertigo that she felt in this position.

"What the hell did you give her, Mila?" Leo muttered.

Mimi wrinkled her eyebrows. *Who is Mila?* Then the words slowly sunk in. She sat up.

"You!" She pointed a finger in Leo's wide eyes and open mouth. "You are the one who drugged me last night! You are the reason that I'm ill!"

Anger replaced relief in an instant as Leo's expression went from light to dark.

"If you pretend like that." Her voice was stone cold. "I won't believe you if you actually need help. Don't cry wolf."

Mimi snarled. Like she cared about that. She wasn't planning to be with Leo long enough for something like this to be needed a second time.

"Answer my question," she demanded. "Did you drug me last night?"

Leo turned her gaze back on the road.

"No."

"No?" Mimi didn't believe her. Not in the least. "I'm not an idiot." She pursed her lips, reveling in the fury that rose within her. Anger was nicer than fear.

She was fed up with the situation now. She wanted to go home, drink a large cup of coffee, and put an ice pack on her head. And then do a lot of sewing.

"I hate you." The words probably meant nothing in Leo's ears. But it felt good to say.

*

"I have to pee."

Leo didn't know whether to laugh or cry. Mimi was already a pain in Leo's ass and they hadn't even left England yet. Nagging, crying, trying to get away. And now needing to pee. One thing was clear, she needed to keep a very close eye on her.

How they were going to get across the English Channel, she still had no idea. How she was going to keep Mimi silent and compliant long enough to even do so was a mystery. A mystery she needed to solve very soon.

"Fine," she said after thinking for a few minutes. "There is a small rest stop ahead. We will walk among the trees and you can find a bush or something. I need to make some phone calls."

"You need further instructions?" The tone in Mimi's voice was taunting.

Leo decided to play with her a little.

"You should be careful, you know." She let her voice lower. "I get paid whether you're alive or not. Accidents can happen."

Mimi let a small gasp escape her and when Leo threw her a look she could see her bottom lip quivering.

Leo smiled a wicked smile, mainly for her own benefit. She had no intention of actually hurting Mimi, but scaring her was both beneficial and fun. If it was possible to scare Mimi into doing what she was told, things would be easier for both of them.

They approached the rest stop and Leo took the next exit. The rest stop was completely empty. Leo felt relief but still parked the car close to the trees, and as far away from the road as possible.

She stopped the car but didn't unlock it at first. She took her phone out of her bag and put it in her pocket. At first she pondered grabbing her gun as well, it was there in the bottom of her bag and would be a great tool for intimidating. But after a moment's consideration, she decided against it. She was both taller and heavier than Mimi, the gun would just be in the way. Especially since she didn't actually have any wish to use it at all. She looked at Mimi.

Mimi was glancing continuously between Leo and her box of fabrics in the back, it almost looked like she was estimating how much she would lose if she ran and left her stuff behind. It was clear that Leo couldn't unlock the doors, get out, and walk to the other side; Mimi would run as soon as her door was opened. She would not get very far, but Leo didn't want to take any chances.

She gestured to Mimi.

"Come here." She pointed toward her lap.

"You creep." Mimi pursed her lips but her eyes were wide and shiny. "What the hell do you want now?"

"Just come here." Leo didn't feel like explaining and reached out to grab a hold of Mimi's wrist. She pulled and knew that Mimi had no choice but to let her be pulled onto the driver's side, into her lap. Mimi kicked and screamed, but it didn't help her. Leo was much stronger and soon she had the small body cradled in her lap. Mimi kept struggling and managed to elbow Leo in the face before the door was pushed open. Leo pushed her out of the door but kept a firm grip on her arm while getting out herself.

"You creep," Mimi repeated as Leo got out of the car after her.

She looked like she was ready to spit in Leo's face but just bit her lip instead.

"Come on." Leo dragged her into the woods, behind some bushes, and let go.

"Don't try anything." She turned around. She didn't want to give Mimi a chance to run away, but she couldn't bear to humiliate Mimi by actually looking.

"Can't I have more privacy than this?"

"No."

Leo had been hoping that Mimi would just do her business and then Leo could make her phone calls. But alas, after the ruffling of clothes, Mimi took off, her steps soft but audible on the leaf and pine needles underground.

"*Allah belanı versin,*" Leo swore to herself in Turkish and ran after her.

Mimi was fast, but she couldn't compete with Leo's much longer legs. After just a few strides, she caught up and tackled Mimi to the ground. She did her best to have them land softly when they went down on the ground together but didn't manage to stop Mimi from banging her head. As annoyed as Leo was with her, she didn't want her to get hurt, and she felt guilty when she heard the small *"oumph"* and *"ouch."* She immediately rolled off the body underneath and helped her up.

Mimi looked up at her, angry tears forming in the corners of her eyes and eventually spilling down her cheeks. She didn't look scared and sad now. Just very, very pissed off. The bump that was forming on her forehead seemed pissed off too.

This is the last thing I need, Leo thought. She doubted that an injured Mimi would be any easier to deal with. Leo expected her to yell or fight, but she didn't. She just followed as Leo lead her back to the car and sat her down. She didn't protest when Leo put the seat belt around her, attached it, and closed the door. Her angry eyes just followed Leo.

Leo locked the door just to be safe, went over to the driver's side, unlocked the car, got inside, and immediately locked them again. Then she leaned over to take a better look at Mimi's head.

It wasn't growing anymore, but it was quite red. Leo touched it as gently as it could, unable not to be worried. Mimi kept her gaze down, arms crossed, and a sour look in her face. It wasn't that Leo cared for her, but she wanted to get the job well done. After all, she had nearly perfect client satisfaction and she wanted to keep it that way. It didn't matter that the package this time was a living, breathing, annoying little spitfire.

"You'll be okay." Leo removed her hand. "Just don't fall asleep for at least 30 minutes and let me know if you're feeling anything strange. Nausea, headache, anything."

"I'm nauseated," Mimi said right away. "I feel like I'm going to faint." In a dramatic fashion she put the back of her hand against her forehead. "Please, I need a hospital."

It was an Oscar-worthy performance, if the conditions for earning an Oscar were overly dramatic and cringe-worthy acting.

"Oh, shut it." Leo took out her phone. "I need to make some phone calls."

Mimi fell silent but the look in her eyes suggested that she was just waiting, biding her time, and sooner or later she would create more trouble for Leo.

Leo needed to forget about her little prisoner for now and quickly dialed Sandra's number. No answer. Leo let the signals run until they stopped. She tried again. Still no answer. She groaned and cut the connection, then dialed Hal's number instead. It was, after all, where she was instructed to bring Mimi. But even without Sandra's instructions, she probably would have anyway.

Hal's farm house was commonly used as a midway stop for anyone driving from Britain and into Europe. Sometimes Sandra's couriers waited there for further instructions, sometimes to negotiate about pay. Originally from Denmark, Hal had lived long enough in France to speak the language fluently. When he didn't pick up the phone either, Leo chose to leave a message in French. Out of habit mostly, but also so that Mimi wouldn't understand.

"*Hi Hal, it's Leo.*" Leo kept her gaze on Mimi. It was always a possibility that Mimi spoke and understood French. "*I have the* package, *and I'm heading to Calais as soon as I can. You can expect me by nightfall if not sooner.*" She hung up.

Mimi was looking at her, but her expression was unreadable and Leo doubted she had understood.

"*Il m'a demandé de te tuer, et vue tout ce que tu m'as fait déjà, je vais prendre mon temps à le faire.*" She decided to test her. She doubted that Mimi could keep her expression as she described the way she could kill her. As she talked, Leo started to feel a bit sick. It didn't matter that Mimi was a bitch, she didn't deserve to die at the hands of Leo. At least she looked more confused than scared.

Satisfied that Mimi didn't understand a word of French, Leo started the car again.

Chapter Four

Mimi felt powerless now, but all it did was piss her off even more. She wasn't stupid, she had been reading the road signs and knew that they were driving toward Dover, and Leo *had* spoken French on the phone. It wasn't hard to understand that Leo was planning to take them to France using the Dover-Calais ferry.

Over my dead body, Mimi thought angrily. Leo could try, but she would make things very hard for her.

Mimi sank back into her seat and looked out of the window. The trees were still flying by.

"Where are you taking me?" No answer. "Where are we going? Could you let me know, please?" She was proud of how demanding her voice sounded, despite swallowing back tears. She focused on Leo. Low-key, as if in the background, she could feel the bump on her head, slowly pulsing.

"We're going to France," Leo said curtly.

Mimi crossed her arms over her chest. "How are you going to pull that off?"

"I'll put you in the trunk if I have to," Leo said without emotion. "But otherwise I was thinking that if you're nice and quiet, we could simply stay in the car."

Mimi gasped when Leo mentioned the trunk. *Leo couldn't seriously think that Mimi would stay quiet during the entire boat trip, did she?*

"I have been drugged," she hurried to say. "I have a bump on my head, I haven't eaten. If you put me in the trunk, at best I'll throw up, at worst I'll slip into a coma."

"Don't be so dramatic."

Leo's calm voice made Mimi want to beat the tranquility out of her face. She did the only thing she could think of.

She started beating on the window, yelling and waving.

"Heeeelp!" She knew that nobody could necessarily hear her, but she hoped to get her signal across. Anyone who saw her now could clearly see that she was in trouble. She tried to get eye contact with other people in the cars, all while making wild gestures.

"Stop it!" Leo sounded strange. "If you continue that, I'm putting you in the trunk." She gripped the wheel so hard, her knuckles were going white.

Mimi looked at her, knowing what she had to do. Using the last of her strength, she lunged forward and grabbed the wheel with both hands. She wasn't sure what the goal was, she just knew that she had to get the car off the road. The car tore violently to the side, and a car behind them honked. She tried to pull the wheel towards her even more, but Leo was both stronger and faster. With a steel grip, she moved the wheel back on course and with her other hand she hit Mimi in the head, pushing her into the window. The car stabilized and they continued forward calmly.

"Fuck, what is wrong with you?" Mimi sank back into her seat, rubbing the side of her forehead. The headache was back in full force, and it was all Leo's fault.

"Ouch."

She barely noticed the car violently turning off the road and stopping at another rest stop.

Leo got up and ran to her side of the car. The passenger door was ripped open, Leo unlocked her seatbelt and then pulled her out with a hard grip on her arm.

"Ouch." Mimi whined as the hold on her wrist hardened. She noticed that Leo was pulling her toward the back of the car, and she dug her heels into the earth, doing anything to fight.

"No, please, please, please, please." She tried to get a hold of anything on the car, and twisted her body. "Please, not the trunk. I won't do it again, I'll be silent. I promise. *Please!*"

"I'm sorry." Leo said while not stopping. "You've given me no choice."

Fear rose within her as Mimi fought even harder, but Leo didn't seem to notice the little punches and kicks. She leaned down, lifted her up, and threw Mimi over her shoulder. She then went to the back of the car, opened the trunk, and placed Mimi inside it.

"You'll never get away with this!" Mimi's eyes were filled with angry tears.

"Yes, I will." Leo's eyes looked sad, but the side of her lips were curling into a smile.

"Bitch." Mimi was adamant that as soon as Leo closed the trunk, she would resume her yelling. She would make so much noise that someone would hear her sooner or later. She would get rescued.

But Leo didn't just close the trunk. She sat down next to Mimi and pulled her head onto her lap. She held Mimi's flailing arms with one hand and brought a vial to her lips with the other.

Mimi didn't want to swallow whatever it was that Leo had just poured into her mouth, but she had no choice. Her head was tilted backwards, secured in the crook of Leo's elbow, and the thick liquid was moving to the back of her throat. It was swallow or drown.

"Good girl," Leo said when Mimi swallowed. She didn't let go.

Mimi squirmed, struggling, but little by little she got drowsy and her movements less forceful.

"What did you do to me?" Her voice sounded strange to her own ears, like it was very far away.

Leo moved her gently off of her lap. The plastic of the trunk was hard against Mimi's back.

"I just gave you something to relax." Leo disappeared from Mimi's line of sight and there was a loud ripping sound.

My textiles!

"Help me." Mimi's voice was weak now and tears dripped from the corner of her eyes. "Anyone." The last word was barely more than a whisper.

Leo came back, holding several pieces of rippled fabric. Mimi's eyes widened when she recognized the pattern.

"You son of a…" Mimi's world turned black.

*

Mimi is such a pain in the ass, Leo thought as she found a free table on the ferry. She expected relief to come now that she was on the ferry and Mimi was safe in the car, but all she felt was an emotion somewhere between worry and guilt. Mimi was indeed annoying, but it hurt her to think of the little person alone in the trunk. Down there, so close to the water. There wasn't a lot of waves today, but the boat still moved slowly from side to side.

At least she is drugged, Leo tried to make herself feel better, but it didn't work. *She can't get seasick.*

Her stomach growled, but she wasn't going to buy anything to eat. Mimi was most likely hungry too. It was best to get some food in her, especially considering all the medication she had ingested in the past 24 hours. She would get them something to eat at Hal's, he lived only 25 minutes from the ferry to the outskirts of Guînes, so they would be there quickly. Mimi should sleep around three hours more, which was plenty of time.

She looked at her phone, there wasn't any signal, naturally, but the ferry had free wifi. She typed a quick email to Sandra, told her that they were making their way across the English Channel. She didn't write that she had given Mimi the sleeping drugs, for some reason she didn't want Sandra to know that Mimi was being a pain. Sandra was ruthless, and Leo didn't want that focus on Mimi. She couldn't even explain why.

Her stomach growled again, and she rubbed it subconsciously. She wondered what had happened. One moment she was seventeen years old and her older lover asked her to, as a favor, carry something across European borders, and in the next moment she was here. Criminal for many years. And now a kidnapper too.

Was she proud of herself?

No. No, she really wasn't.

Chapter Five

Mimi's world was dark and moist, and the air was stale. At first she thought that she was dead, but then her body started waking up. It felt like little ants wandered up and down her arms and legs. She wanted to move, to stretch, to take away the awful stiff feeling in the leg closest to the floor. *The floor?* Where was she? Her arms were tied together in front of her body.

You're in the trunk of a car. Reality came and smacked her in the face. Breath forced its way through her airways and she cried. She *hated* small enclosed spaces.

The second thing Mimi noticed was the fury concentrating in her core and spreading out until all she could see was red. She couldn't remember another time when she had been this angry. Not when her store had been robbed. Not when her dad had forbidden her to date someone as a teenager. Not when her friend had insulted her sewing. She had never been this furious, and all the flaming anger had gathered in the pit of her stomach to focus on one person. *Leo.* If it was the last thing Mimi ever did, Leo would pay for what she had done. And she remembered everything that Leo had done.

Anger was good. Anger kept her from focusing too much on the bumpy ride and how scared she actually was. It helped her from crying out of fear, panicking, or wondering if she would ever again get to see her home. She tried to ignore how the walls seemed to close in around her or how her nails instinctively dug into plastic carpet she was lying on.

The car came to a halt.

Mimi held her breath as a car door opened, closed, and steps came closer. The trunk opened and light flooded in. Mimi had to squint, but she didn't need her vision to know that it was Leo. There was no denying the now familiar hands that were pulling her into an upright position and undoing the fabric holding her hands together. There was also no denying the long black hair or the slight scent of soap and mint. And cigarettes. Mimi still had never seen Leo smoke but her scent gave her off.

"Hé Léo! C'est toi?" A man's voice said, making Mimi wish she had paid more attention in the French lessons of her youth.

"Ouais. Attends que je l'emmène à l'intérieur, et là on peut parler."

Mimi bit her tongue, doing her best not to complain at being handled so casually. She didn't want Leo to drug her again. Next time she screamed for help, it would be without Leo in the vicinity. She was picked up rather gently, and she forced herself to lie inert in Leo's arms as she was carried inside a building and a door slammed shut.

"Descends-la à la cave. Il y a une chambre fait exprès pour les « paquets » de ce genre," the man said. Mimi turned her face and tried to squint through half-way closed eyelids in an attempt to get a better look, but Leo turned her around.

"Tu 'm'ouvres la porte? J'ai les mains pleines." That was Leo. It was unnerving to not understand what they were saying.

A door creaked and Mimi opened her eyes just in time to see a stairway leading downwards. Playing unconscious became less important as Mimi's mind flooded with panic.

"No, please. Don't put me down there." She was still weak from the drugs but did her best to squirm.

She opened her eyes in time to see Leo's surprised expression. She was put down on the floor, but Leo kept an arm around her shoulders as if worried she would fall without them.

They looked at each other. Mimi wanted to see sympathy in Leo's gaze. Neither of them spoke.

"Please," Mimi said eventually. "I'll do anything, I'll…" Mimi was really ready to do anything. Being locked in a basement was not something she wanted to experience ever again. Her dad's preferred method of punishment was only one of the reasons she had moved from home.

Something looking like sadness passed in Leo's eyes, but then her mouth pressed into a thin line, and she turned Mimi around without answering her. She pushed her forward gently but kept the hold of her shoulders to stop her from falling. Mimi didn't want to, but she didn't see any other choice. She wasn't strong enough to fight Leo off, she just wasn't.

"Please," she tried one last time when they reached the end of the stairs. *Don't cry in front of Leo, don't cry in front of Leo, don't cry in front of Leo. Don't show any weakness.*

Leo pushed her through a door. Whereas the stairway had been lit up, the new room had no source of light, even a window. It was pitch black, and Mimi felt like a cold hand took hold of her throat.

Before Leo had had a chance to push Mimi through the door and close it, Mimi turned around and dug her fingers into Leo's leather jacket.

"Don't leave me here." She felt tears of fear travelling down her cheeks for the second time this day. "I'll die if you leave me here."

"I'm sorry." Leo sounded genuine, but it meant nothing when she ripped Mimi's hands away and took a step backwards. "I'm really sorry."

Mimi didn't care about Leo's apologies. As the door closed, she fell to the floor and wailed.

*

When Leo came up the stairs, Hal was sitting by the table working on his embroidery. It wasn't the manliest of tasks, but he had been doing it for a long time and Leo didn't question it. She had known Hal for almost as long as she had been working for Sandra. It had been well enough time for Leo to get used to a man with sideburns, tattoo covered arms, and a passion for fine needle work.

She sat down in front of him at the table and popped a piece of gum in her mouth. God, she needed a smoke. She groaned and pulled her fingers through her hair. Maybe it was getting too long after all, she should probably cut it—

She groaned again. She was well aware that she was focusing on menial things, anything so she didn't have to think about Mimi all alone in the dark. That room was terrifying, even to Leo. And Leo wasn't plagued by whatever fear of basements Mimi clearly has.

"*What's wrong with you?*" Hal said, sticking to French.

"*How long has Sandra been dealing with humans?*" Leo couldn't keep the disgust out of her voice and saw no reason to beat around the bush.

"*Does it surprise you?*" Hal's eyebrows went up. "*You've been working for Sandra for over ten years. Nobody knows her as well as you do.*"

Leo got up from her chair and went to the window, staring at the small garden outside. It was true what Hal was saying. She had known Sandra for a long time, and she was familiar with her ruthlessness, her greed, and her selfishness, and yet she had thought that there were some things that were too sinister, too cold, even for her boss.

"*It doesn't happen often.*" When Leo still hadn't said anything, Hal continued. "*But sometimes, if the client and the price is right, she'll transport people too.*"

"*Transport? Ha.*" Leo snorted. "*It's kidnapping and you know it.*"

There was a small clink when Hal put his embroidery down. He came to stand next to her by the window. The day was slowly turning into evening. Shadows were forming on the lawn. Leo wanted time to go faster. Every minute that Mimi was down there was another minute that Leo couldn't fully relax.

"*You've transported drugs,*" Hal said. "*You've transported illegal animals and plants, stolen art, illicit documents, the list goes on, why would you —*"

"*Because she's a person,*" Leo snapped.

She could feel Hal staring at her but refused to look up.

"*Are you upset about kidnapping in general, or about this woman specifically?*"

Leo refused to answer.

"*Who is paying for her anyway?*" She asked instead. "*Where is she going?*"

"I can't answer that for you," Hal answered. *"Sandra was supposed to send me an address, she usually does in cases like this. But she's been out of touch."*

"Out of touch?" Sandra hadn't answered her either.

"We're probably going to have to keep Mimi here for a couple of days."

Leo's heart sped up imagining Mimi's tear stricken face downstairs in the dark basement.

"She can't stay down there." Leo did her best to sound calm, but it was hard to keep the anger out of her voice. *"I won't allow it. She needs a proper bed. Food. She needs to be able to use a bathroom, take a shower, be—"*

Hal held up his hand and she fell silent.

"I have a good thing going here, Leo. I can't jeopardize it for—" They locked eyes and whatever he saw there made him nod. *"She's your responsibility. You don't want her to stay in the basement? Fine, then she can stay with you, in your room. We'll handcuff her to a bed."*

Leo wanted to thank him, but she kept her facial expression impassive. She was already out of line making demands for somebody who shouldn't matter. She tried to not let the waves of relief she was feeling come up to the surface. *It just means I'm human,* she thought, *it's normal to care about others.*

"I'll put handcuffs that you can use on the dresser." Hal patted her shoulder and left to prepare the room.

As soon as he had gone up the stairs, Leo headed for the basement door. She ran down the stairs and undid the lock. She couldn't wait to get Mimi out of there.

She opened the door slowly and, before she could realize what was happening, a small body came out of nowhere and leapt right at her. It made Leo stagger for a moment, but she gathered her balance quickly and reached for Mimi, trying to envelop her into a hug. Mimi struggled and managed to kick Leo in the shin. With a yell, Mimi set off, but instead of aiming for the stairs, she ran the other way, further into the basement. She was trapped, and all Leo had to do was run up to her. She grabbed hold of Mimi's arm, tugged hard, and Mimi came flying into her arms. She crossed Mimi's arms over her chest and pulled her close so her back was pressed against Leo.

"Fuck you." Mimi tried to move and Leo was finding it increasingly hard to keep her still. On a strange surge of strength, Mimi tore free, turned around in Leo's arms, and sank her teeth into Leo's upper arm.

Leo grunted in pain and swept her leg forward to knock Mimi off her feet. As soon as Mimi fell forward, Leo grabbed a hold of her waist and, with much difficulty, threw her over her shoulder. Mimi wailed like a banshee and slammed her fists into Leo's back.

"Let me go! Let me go!"

She could do whatever she wanted, Leo didn't care. She carried the screaming and crying woman up one set of stairs, then a second. Her arm was aching, the bite that Mimi had left tingling in a disconcerting way.

"In here!" Hal called out when she was on the second floor.

Leo followed Hal's voice and brought the screaming and kicking Mimi into the room. She threw her on the bed and quickly handcuffed her to the headboard.

"Let me go! Help! Somebody help me!" Mimi's voice was loud.

Leo and Hal shared a look. Hal's face was turning red.

"Make her shut up, someone will hear her." He looked down on her, his eyes filled with such indifference it

made Leo's insides run cold. What kind of people did she work with?

"Help!" Mimi called again. "Help, help, help, help—"

Hal ran up to her and punched her hard in the jaw.

"Shut up." He slapped her again, as if needing his hand to convey the message twice.

Mimi yelped, fell silent, and looked up at her captors with watery eyes, her lip now split and bleeding. The sight struck something within Leo's core. She had been a criminal for over ten years, had hit, been hit, and seen more than just slaps and punches. And still, she couldn't stand it. *I did this.* It took Leo a minute to realize what she was feeling. It was *guilt.*

"Hal!" Leo dragged him out of the room. Inside the room, Mimi was sobbing loudly.

"*You...*" Leo breathed hard and saw red. She felt like delivering a punch of her own between Hal's stupid eyes. "*You will not hit her again, is that clear?*"

"*What's wrong with you?*" Hal pushed something plastic in her hand. "*She's going to be trouble. Knock her out.*"

He left her outside the bedroom and walked downstairs, his heavy steps echoing inside the little house.

Leo stood still for a couple of minutes, staring at the bottle of sleeping pills in her hand. She didn't care what Hal thought about her anymore, hitting Mimi was not okay on any level.

She was over this job now. She wanted to go to Portugal or Spain or Greece. Maybe Turkey. She wanted to lay down on a beach somewhere with a drink in one hand and a french fry in the other. But before she could go on a well-deserved vacation, she had other things to deal with first.

She didn't go back in Mimi's room right away, instead she went downstairs to the kitchen and grabbed some bread and cheese. She also grabbed a bottle of water and a kitchen towel. Carrying her loot, Leo went back upstairs.

Mimi was lying on the bed, her legs crossed as if making up for the fact that one of her arms was spread and stuck to the bedpost. Her black hair was messy, and when she looked at Leo there was pure hatred in her eyes.

Leo put the things on the dresser, wet the towel, and went toward Mimi.

"Don't touch me." Mimi's tone was harsh, but her bottom lip was quivering.

"I'm not going to hurt you." Leo wanted to be unemotional, but she couldn't will her movements to be anything but gentle. She couldn't blame Mimi's fear, Leo had done nothing but abhorrent things to her. Mimi's fear was nothing but justified.

She dabbed the towel on Mimi's split lip, cleaned up the blood, and wiped away the stray tears. All while Mimi's angry eyes never left her.

When Leo was satisfied that Mimi was clean, she got up, grabbed the food from the dresser, and presented it to Mimi.

At first it looked like Mimi wanted to protest, but then her stomach rumbled and she held out her free hand to accept the bread that Leo had stuffed the cheese into. She ate it with gusto while never breaking eye contact with Leo. Her eyes were red, but responsive, which was a relief. Mimi had been drugged several times in a row and bumped her head, so Leo was happy to see that she seemed okay, albeit very pissed off.

When Mimi had swallowed the last bite, Leo turned around and reached for the bottle of water and the plastic casing with the pills. When she faced Mimi again, Mimi's eyes widened and she shook her head.

"Over my dead body," she said through gritted teeth. "I'm serious, you're going to have to kill me. I'm not taking any more pills."

Leo groaned out of frustration. It was true that she didn't want to drug her. Not again. Not if she didn't want to. *Come on,* her brain said, *what's wrong with you? Just drug the bitch. You know she'll be trouble.* It was weakness, Leo realized that, this not wanting to drug her. But she couldn't. *It's just because you're worried that she's going to slip into a coma.*

"You make another peep." She held up one finger in front of Mimi's face, letting her fill in the gap.

"Yes, yes, if I make another peep you can knock me out again, I get it." Mimi's voice was croaky. An angelic smile spread over her features, but a dangerous sparkle remained in her eyes. Leo knew that Mimi was unstable and untrustworthy. But she felt compelled to give her another chance.

She checked the handcuffs one last time.

"I'll be back," she said. Then she left the room.

I hate this job, she thought as she went down the stairs. She didn't know why she was even staying anymore. *I got Mimi to Hal's, nobody can ask more of me. I'm not cut up for this job anyway. I'm nowhere near ruthless enough to kidnap people.*

If Mila had been the one to kidnap Mimi, she would have just drugged her and put her in the trunk from the beginning. No fuss. And Mimi wouldn't have hit her head falling on the ground. She would have stayed in the basement which meant that Hal wouldn't have hit her. In one way Mimi would have been safer that way. Under Mila's brutal, but watchful, eye.

Then again Mila would also have thrown Mimi in the basement, not bothered by her terror or her screams. No, Leo was happy that she had screwed up Mila's operation. She was happy that she was the one who had kidnapped Mimi. It wasn't that she cared for Mimi, the little bitch. Leo would be happy to see her go when the job was over. But no one should be treated worse than necessary. Mimi was human and she deserved to be treated as such.

She entered the kitchen. Hal was by the sink, drinking something from a bottle. Leo felt fury run through her veins when she looked at him. *Get a grip, Leo.* She opened her mouth, wanting to make up, when a scream from the *outside* made her mouth drop open.

"Putain!" Hal threw his drink into the sink, rushed past Leo, and headed for the stairs.

Fuck! Leo set off after him right away. She didn't want to know how Mimi was managing to scream so that it could be heard from the outside.

When they ran into Mimi's room, they found her practically hanging out of the now-opened window, screaming for help. The only thing holding her back was the handcuffs that she had stretched as far as the chain would go.

"Close the window!" Hal went straight for Mimi, grabbed her, and pulled her back into the room again.

Leo ran up to the window and slammed it shut. She felt like bringing her fists to Mimi's face herself now. She couldn't believe that Mimi had actually done something so stupid. They would have no choice but to drug her now. And Leo was also angry with herself, she couldn't believe she had been so stupid as to give Mimi a chance to stay quiet.

"I don't care what you think." Hal was holding her down, pressing a large hand to Mimi's mouth. *"I'm giving her something. Come here and hold her."*

It was clear that Mimi had no plans on cooperating. When Hal got up, she flailed her one free hand and kicked with her legs. Leo ducked two kicks before jumping forward and grabbing hold of her. She twisted her around, sat down on the bed, and held her against her body.

"Let me go!" Mimi arched her body, trying to force Leo to lose her grip.

It didn't work this time. Leo held her against her body, holding her arms and enveloping Mimi's legs with her own. Mimi was stuck and angry growling noises escaped from her mouth. Sounding more wild animal than human.

Hal returned to the room, came forward, and forced her mouth open by pressing on her cheeks with his fingers. He proceeded to pour both pills and water in her throat. She spluttered and coughed and Leo held her closer.

"Swallow," she whispered in Mimi's ear. "Swallow before you drown." *Please Mimi.*

Mimi pushed out air through her nostrils and looked at Leo with hatred in her eyes as she swallowed on the next inhale. She started sobbing again, loudly and violently. Leo could feel each sob and it broke her soul. The whole situation was just *wrong*. Leo wanted to comfort the woman in her arms and instead she was the one hurting her.

Out of Hand

"It would have been better to keep her in the basement." Hal looked straight at Leo who was still on the bed. *"I'm making dinner if you want some."* He left.

Since he was gone, Leo allowed herself to hold Mimi until her sobs subsided. Then she gently pushed her off her lap and got up from the bed. Mimi's eyes were still open, but her gaze was turned away from Leo. Her chest heaved up and down; her mouth open to let air out in small panicked gasps. She was the very vision of a broken woman.

You're a monster, Leo. It was the truth. It didn't matter what she had done before this. This, Mimi's kidnapping, was the worst crime that Leo had ever committed. And would ever commit. *I'm never doing this again.*

Leo grabbed a chair and sat down next to the bed. She wanted to apologize, to say something, but there was nothing she could say. Instead, she sat silently and watched Mimi cry herself to sleep.

Chapter Six

Pound, pound, pound, pound. There was a second heartbeat in Mimi's head. A painful, tedious heartbeat. She opened her eyes slowly and peeked under half-closed eyelids. Everything was blurry and her eyes wouldn't focus. She closed them completely again and focused on her other senses.

She sucked in air through her mouth, wanting to call for help, but also not daring to. She also wasn't entirely sure her voice would hold. She cleared her throat. She needed to do something. Anything.

I'm Mimi, she reminded herself, *I'm not helpless. I'm not pathetic. I don't get* fucking *kidnapped.* She didn't let people walk all over her. Mimi knew who she was. She just needed to remind the rest of the world.

Little by little the world became clearer, and she was suddenly aware of two people arguing loudly downstairs. She forced her eyes open and looked toward the door.

It was that man and Leo, that much she understood, but it was otherwise impossible for her to understand what they were saying.

Are they arguing about me? Mimi closed her eyes again, wanting to hide from the world. It was like she had stepped out of her own life and into a fever dream. Kidnapped. Did that actually happen to real people? Where they going to ask her parents for ransom?

Mimi snorted. *As if my dad would pay ransom for his screwed up disappointment of a daughter.*

"*Ça m'emmerde.*" Leo yelled. "*Je sors fumer!*" Her voice sounded louder, closer, as if she was standing in the hallway, right underneath the stairs. Her yell was followed by the door being slammed shut.

Mimi lifted her head again, ignoring the dizziness.

"Leo?" Her voice was weak.

Did Leo just leave? Had she just left Mimi by herself?

Dread filled her and she fell back against the mattress, crying in terror. As angry she had been with Leo, and as much as she hated her, she instinctively knew she was much safer with her than the man who had struck her twice. She had started to learn Leo's limits and what Leo was willing to do. Anybody else felt a thousand time more uncertain.

"Leo?" She tried again.

There were steps in the stairs, and Mimi hurried to close her eyes, pretending to still be asleep.

"I know you're awake." Apparently the man of the house *did* speak a language other than French. "You can't fool me."

Mimi kept her eyes closed, but she knew from her elevated heartbeat and faster breath that it was quite obvious that she wasn't sleeping. She opened her eyes.

"I'm hungry. You need to bring me something to eat." When in doubt, make demands. It was something Mimi had learned early. Most people did as you asked as long as you faked authority well enough.

The man laughed and looked at her, crossing his arms. He wasn't looking at her like a predator, just very amused, like Mimi had told a funny joke.

"Where is Leo?"

"Out for a smoke." His words caused waves of relief to wash over Mimi, but she didn't change the expression on her face. Leo hadn't left—not completely.

"I'm hungry," she repeated. "I know you have food here."

The man shook his head.

"You're cuffed to a bed," he said. "What makes you think that you have any power here?" He said it matter-of-factly. He wasn't taunting Mimi, he seemed to test her. As if he was curious to what she would say next.

"I've got low blood sugar," she tried. "You need to keep me fed otherwise your…" she looked for the appropriate word, "… *customers* won't pay for me. Wouldn't want to hand me over undernourished, hurt, dying—"

"Be quiet, Mimi." Leo entered. "Don't anger the man of the house more than you have to."

Leo! Mimi did her damndest to not show any sign of relief in her face. She pursed her lips and lifted one of her eyebrows.

"I need food." She kept her eyes on Leo.

"I'll bring you something." She turned to the man who was still staring at Mimi. "You coming?"

He nodded.

"Not fish." Mimi called after them.

She smirked to herself. When in doubt, make demands. And Mimi was very good at making demands.

*

Leo's eyes fluttered open. It was nighttime, and she was sleeping on the bed across from Mimi's. It was still dark outside, but the light was still on in the hallway and the room was dim. She sat up and rubbed her knuckles into her eyes. She had dreamt about her dad, a man she hadn't thought about in many years. The dad who had chased her for fun, hugged her, and affectionately called her "Nora" was a memory so old that it might as well have never happened. She still missed him, and yet she refused to get in touch with him. She couldn't show him what she had become. She would never be able to bear the disappointment in his eyes. It was better this way.

"Help..."

A soft murmur from the other bed made Leo look up.

Mimi was wiggling on top of the covers. Leo wasn't sure if Mimi was just uncomfortable, or if she was having a bad dream.

She got up and walked over to Mimi's bed. Mimi cried and thrashed from side to side. Leo wanted to help, but there wasn't anything she could do. Mimi had been drugged again after eating, and Leo wasn't even sure she could wake her up properly. Mimi was stuck in whatever nightmare she was having.

"Help." Mimi sounded so helpless it broke Leo's heart. At that moment, she didn't even question it, she just knew that she would have done absolutely anything to help her.

Mimi turned violently to the side and flashed her eyes open. At first glance her eyes looked the same, blackish brown, but in the same time they were completely different. Mimi just wasn't home. Her eyes were lacking that spark that was life. Leo bit her lip. *Why do you care? You don't care about Mimi?* Leo shook her head. She didn't.

"I want to go home." Mimi's words were slurred. "I don't want to be here anymore."

"I know." Leo sat down on the bed and stroked the top of her head.

Mimi wasn't crying, but her eyes were shining as if filled with tears as she looked up at Leo. Her lip was still swollen and her cheek was red from the way Hal had hit her earlier.

"You have blue eyes." She looked straight at Leo.

"Umm... yeah?" Leo didn't know what to reply. There was no way Mimi could see her eyes in the dark.

"I used to have a sister," Mimi said and yawned. "Her name was... was... was..." She yawned and closed her eyes. Leo pulled a couple of stray hairs from her face. She was about to get up and go to her own bed when Mimi opened her mouth again.

"Her favorite color was blue," she said. "When I look into your eyes, I almost understand why." With that she closed her eyes and started snoring. Leo stared at her. Shook her head. Then she went back to bed.

Chapter Seven

During the next two days, guilt crept through Leo's body like poison. With every little dose they fed Mimi, Leo had been poisoning herself too. Mimi was kept docile and easy to deal with, which had been 'the right choice.' It was still wrong.

She was relieved that it was over now. Hal had received a phone call early this morning, and Sandra was on her way. It was puzzling why Sandra hadn't called Leo directly, but Leo didn't think about it. The important thing was that the whole situation was over now. Leo could finally go back to her old life, delivering dead cargo and not having to worry. Or deal with bitchy, troublesome, annoying…. Leo sighed. She should have been anticipating Sandra's visit and instead she was dreading it. What would happen to Mimi once Sandra took over? Leo didn't want to think about it.

Sandra was arriving any minute now, and Leo went into Mimi's room to look at her one last time. She wasn't going to miss her, and she was happy that the job was done, but for the past three days she had been in charge of the pitiful creature that was passed out on the bed. For three days she had fed her and cared for her. *Made sure she was safe.* Leo snorted at the thought. Mimi hadn't been safe since somebody had put a contract on her head. But Leo had done her best with what she had been given.

Mimi looked vulnerable on her back, not able to have a say on who looked at her or came into her room. Leo brushed some stray black hairs, and also picked up some crumbs that were still in Mimi's palm. Being drugged didn't just make Mimi loopy, sleepy, and docile. It also made her very hungry. Any time she had been even remotely conscious she had asked for food. Although maybe that was just Mimi's natural state. Leo didn't know. After all, she didn't actually know Mimi.

"Little spitfire." The words were out before Leo even thought them. She hoped that whatever happened next, nobody would hurt her. Or lock her in a basement. *Or starve her*. Leo couldn't help but feel worried.

The world seemed so dangerous all of a sudden. Why was there a contract in the first place? Who wanted her? Was it for ransom? And if it was for ransom, what happened with Mimi if nobody paid it? The world was so dangerous for Mimi, Leo couldn't stand it.

The door downstairs opened and closed. Sandra had arrived. Leo gave Mimi's hand a final squeeze, then she headed downstairs.

She couldn't help how her heart beat just a little bit faster at the prospect of meeting Sandra face to face again. It didn't matter that Leo was no longer a blue-eyed young woman with an uncanny ability to pick locks, lie her way out of difficult situations, and eager to get away from under her parents' thumb. It didn't matter that in the past fifteen years, they had both changed. Sandra was older now, with strays of silver in her otherwise black hair and lines around her eyes and mouth that Leo had never gotten to explore.

None of it mattered, when she reached the end of the stairs she reverted back into that same young woman. She stood her ground even as she wanted to throw herself into Sandra's arms. It didn't matter how old she got, she still craved Sandra's attention and approval. She couldn't remember how long it was since they had last met face to face. A year at least. Probably more. At another time, Leo would have hugged her, but it wasn't appropriate. Even if Leo had managed to get Mimi to Hal's, she had at first fucked the whole thing up by not letting Mila do her job. There was no telling how pleased Sandra would actually be with her.

"Do you ladies want some time alone or…?" Sandra and Leo both turned their heads and looked at Hal who was standing in the doorway to the kitchen.

"Yes, please." Sandra waved at him in a dismissive gesture. "Go and spend some time on your embroidery."

She put her arm around Leo's shoulders, despite being much shorter, and led her into the living room. The action wasn't warm but forceful. And when they sat down on the sofa, Leo was sweating. For a moment Leo could forget about everything else, the only thing that existed was Sandra and her obvious disapproval of Leo.

"You gave me a lot of trouble. I have never had an agent leave me the way Mila wanted to do." Her tone of voice was harsh. Her teacher voice. "What you did, it ruined a lot of well laid plans."

"I know." Leo felt empty inside. "I'm sorry."

"Thank you." Sandra's words made her look up. The look in her eyes and tone of her voice had turned angel-wing soft. She put her hand on Leo's. "I know this isn't your type of job, but you delivered."

Her sweet words made goosebumps trickle down Leo's spine. Her heart sped up.

"I will never do anything like this again." Leo had to say it, even if they were said hurriedly and with not much authority. She had to say it before Sandra's touch and her gentle gaze made Leo forget everything. Like it had all other times.

"You'll be paid handsomely." Sandra flashed her teeth in a brilliant smile. "You'll get Mila's share and a little bit extra. Once the job is done."

"Once the job is done?"

"The father is having trouble parting with his money," Sandra waved dismissively with one of her hands. "He has demanded that he speaks with his daughter. I have managed to stall him, but in the next few days you should call him." She took a phone out of her pocket. "Here, use it and toss it out after. His number is already saved on the phone. But don't use the phone until I tell you too. Once the money has been transferred, Mimi needs to be delivered to her dad's house in Berlin within a few hours."

"A ransom?" Leo had suspected it, but it still wasn't believable. If Mimi had rich parents in Germany, what was she doing living in a shady part of London? She didn't look or sound German. The rich parents Leo could believe, however. It explained the spoiled rich girl behavior.

"Yes," Sandra said calmly. "A ransom. We don't usually do jobs like these, but the client is very important to me." She stretched her back, let go of Leo's hand, and made it clear that she was ready to get up. "Will you drive her to Berlin on Thursday?"

Thursday was more than a couple of days away. Leo shook her head.

"I don't want to stay here for another three days," she said.

Sandra relaxed back in the chair again, crossing her legs.

"Hal is not going to agree to look after her himself." Her voice was somewhat demanding and apathetic in the same time. "Well, I guess I can ask Mila again, or Ludvig, or one of the others."

"Will I still get paid?" Leo eyed her suspiciously, she couldn't help but feel like she was getting played.

"Of course, why wouldn't you?" Sandra said. "Not as much, but you can make that up with other agent later, the one that will come for her."

"Maybe I should stay." Leo bit her lip. *What is wrong with you? Just take the money and go.*

Sandra threw her a look and uncrossed her legs.

"Developed a liking for our little prisoner?" She smiled teasingly. "From what I have heard of her, I wouldn't have pegged her as your type."

"Don't be stupid," Leo said. "I just want the whole paycheck." That wasn't the whole truth, but Leo wasn't about to confess that she worried about Mimi. Especially in the hands of one of the others.

They stood up.

"I'll deliver her on Thursday." It was a relief to make the decision. "Just send me the address."

Sandra needed to make a few phone calls, so Leo, dismissed, went to the kitchen to grab herself a glass of water. She couldn't believe what she had just done. What she had just offered to do. She had wanted to go back to her regular life, not continuing this… farce.

She sighed and opened the fridge.

"So I gather she's staying for a few more days?"

Leo turned around, a glass in her hand. Hal looked and sounded murderous, his mouth a thin line, his biceps tensing. The image was ruined by the white cloth adorned with different colored threads that was hanging from one of his hands.

Leo sighed again and took a sip of the water.

"*Another three nights,*" she said once she had swallowed.

"*That's unacceptable.*" His eyes darkened. "*We can't keep drugging her and she won't stay calm if she's not drugged. I won't keep her here.*" He turned toward the door to the living room. "*Sandra, do you hear me?*"

Leo couldn't exactly blame him. Even if his house wasn't in the middle of the city, he still had neighbors on both sides. Keeping Mimi here was risky.

"*I'm not going to pretend like I don't understand you.*" Sandra entered the kitchen again, pocketing her phone. She returned Hal's gaze calmly and seemed to be thinking deeply. "*I also understand that you've been drugging her almost non-stop for the past two days. While that's been necessary, it's hardly ideal. I suppose the best option is to take her somewhere where she can scream as much as she wants.*"

"*Where?*" Leo finished her beer and put the empty bottle in the sink.

"I have a farmhouse near Strasbourg." Sandra smiled at Leo. "I assume you remember it. It's probably dusty and not really fit to live in. But it's desolate and has both water and electricity."

Leo did remember it even though she hadn't been there for a very long time. The last time she had been there, Sandra and she… no, she didn't want to think about that. She also didn't feel like returning there without Sandra and with Mimi, but at least she would have no problem finding it.

*

When Leo returned upstairs, Mimi lay still, her eyes closed, her countenance pale. Apart from the steady rise and fall her chest, she was lying completely still, her eyes open and staring at the ceiling.

"Have you come to make me sleep again?" She asked without moving her gaze.

"Only if I have to." Leo stayed by the door, observing her.

Mimi looked so small, her skin like porcelain, like a doll. It looked like she had lost a bit of weight. In the next following days, Leo was going to be more careful about feeding her.

"I don't want you to." Mimi sobbed. "I don't want to sleep anymore."

Leo said nothing. After a while Mimi lifted her head and looked at Leo. "Am I going now? Is my ransom paid?"

Leo stopped to just look at her.

"You know about the ransom?"

"My dad is rich." Mimi laid back again and closed her eyes. "I was guessing."

"It's going to be a few more days," Leo said. "Then I'm going to take you back to your parents."

"Ha! You say that like if it's a good thing." Mimi laughed mirthlessly.

Leo didn't ask her to clarify. It wasn't any of her business. Instead, she left Mimi and went to the room across the hall to get her gun and her bag. She usually kept her bag in the same room as she slept, but even with Mimi being drugged she didn't dare to have her weapon in there.

Gun in hand, she returned to Mimi. She held her gun out and Mimi's eyes widened.

"I'm not allowed to kill you," Leo said. "But if you cause trouble, I won't hold back from injuring you. My gun is loaded, and if I have to, I will shoot."

Mimi swallowed and nodded.

"If you promise to behave, I won't drug you." Leo didn't take pleasure in Mimi's wide mouth and scared eyes. But she didn't want to have to drug her, she didn't want to have to hurt her or tie her up. She just couldn't think of a better way to keep Mimi from harm than to simply scare her. She ignored how every word made her kind of sick. "We're going to another place. Will you behave or should I place you in the trunk from the beginning?"

"I'll behave." Mimi sounded defeated, her weary voice tugging on Leo's heartstrings.

As terribly annoying as Mimi had been before, she had also seemed so much more alive. Leo hoped that whatever happened after Thursday, Mimi would snap back to her own self once she was back home. The thought that Leo had broken her completely was too painful to bear.

But she believed her. Mimi had learned a painful lesson while cooped up at Hal's, and Leo doubted she would cause her more trouble from now on.

"I'll get the car ready."

Leo gathered the rest of her things and went downstairs. She stopped by the kitchen and placed her bag on the table. She then went to the fridge and started helping herself to a couple of beers and a package of sausages. She put them in her bag. She had every intention of somehow going grocery shopping soon, but she wanted to be prepared in case she didn't get a chance to before dinner. Mimi had promised to behave, so Leo thought it was only right that she would keep her fed in return.

"Here are the keys for my place in Strasbourg." Sandra handed her a set of keys attached to a small plastic nightingale. "There is a basement where you can —" Leo shook her head. "Well, there are several bedrooms too. Just take your pick."

"Why do you still keep that old farmhouse?" Leo had to ask. Sandra clearly didn't use it. She had bought it while her husband was still alive.

"Even if my husband and I never did settle down in France like we wanted when we bought it, I can't make myself sell it." The words were said without emotion.

"Fair enough." Leo picked up her bag and threw it over her shoulder. "We'll be going now. Just going to leave our bag in the car, then I'll go and get... her."

"Change cars," Sandra said hurriedly. "Hal will deal with the car you came in."

"Use the blue Volvo." Hal came into the kitchen and threw her a pair of car keys.

Leo caught them mid-air. Then she took out the keys for Mimi's car. She looked at them for a moment before, reluctantly, put them on the table in front of her. It felt wrong giving away Mimi's car like that.

She went outside and put her bag in the backseat. She would have put it in the trunk but needed to keep it vacant, just in case. She left the passenger seat open and after turning around, headed toward the house in quick strides. Now that plans were drawn, she was eager to get Mimi and just leave.

She opened the door and ran straight into Sandra who had a hurried look on her face. Leo apologized and stepped to the side. Sandra smiled for a nanosecond and pressed a quick kiss to Leo's cheek.

"I have to run, sorry." Her words were hasty and her gaze evasive. "I'll text you the address in a couple of days."

Leo could only nod. There was something agitated in Sandra's eyes. But her gait was calm.

"Sandra?" Leo couldn't help it. Curiosity had gotten the better of her. "How much is the ransom?"

"Five million euro." Sandra turned around.

"That's a lot."

"It's not my place to question the numbers," Sandra said without blinking. "I need to go."

She blew one last kiss at Leo, and then she waltzed down the street, looking as carefree as ever. If she was taking a bus, or being picked up, or even had a car of her own somewhere, Leo didn't know.

Chapter Eight

When Leo came to get her, Mimi wanted to kick her teeth in. She wanted to bite and scratch and kick until Leo would have no choice but to let her go. She tried to lift her arms to fight back, but they were heavy and she whimpered as Leo pulled her into a sitting position.

Mimi hadn't given up that she would one day be free. But for her to get free, she needed to gather her strength.

"I know you're tired." With Leo's firm grip on her upper arms, she was suddenly standing up. "You can sleep in the car."

She was kept ahead of Leo as they went down the stairs and out of the door. *Leo should have blindfolded me,* she thought as they approached the driveway. It was really ridiculous. Mimi could see everything. She smirked, Leo would one day pay. And so would that man. They would *all* pay.

"We have a little bit over four hours to the place we'll be staying." Leo pulled her toward a car Mimi didn't recognize.

"What about my car?" Mimi dug her heels into the dirt and tried to stop Leo from pushing her into the passenger seat.

"We're taking this car now." Leo's tone was calm.

She didn't forcibly push Mimi into the seat and instead just enveloped her between the car door and her own body and waited for Mimi to sit down of her own accord. Even though it was nice to not be pushed, Mimi felt another wave of rage as she sat down and inhaled deeply. Leo leaned forward and fastened Mimi's seatbelt.

"I want my things." Mimi said. "I have fabrics valued for over sixty pounds in there. And my sewing machine. I need them."

Leo locked eyes with her for a moment, then she looked up as if checking that no one was watching. She got up and to Mimi's surprise and joy, Leo went over to her car and got Mimi's things from the back. Leo put them safely in the back of the Volvo and then came to sit next to Mimi.

"Thank you," Mimi whispered, her gaze on her lap. *Why did you thank her, you idiot? It's the* least *she can do, no?*

Leo didn't answer.

*

"So have you been doing this for long?" Mimi was proud that her words weren't slurred. She had too many drugs running through her system.

The look that Leo gave her was priceless, but Mimi ignored it. What was kidnapping 101? *Make yourself appear human to your kidnapper.* Strike up a friendship. Maybe she could become friendly with Leo, and Leo would let her go. After all, Leo had gotten her the sewing machine. And the fabrics. Surely there was a heart in there somewhere. Maybe her soft side could be reached if Mimi played her cards right and acted obediently.

"Yes," Leo said after a little while, returning her gaze to the road. "I usually move less vocal packages though."

Mimi tried to laugh about it but couldn't. Leo hadn't just made a joke.

"How old are you then?"

Leo gave her another look.

"Thirty-two."

"I thought you were younger." Mimi's heart pounded. She hated making small talk with her kidnapper. "I'm twenty-five." She thought for a moment. "So what did you do before this?"

"Are you planning on asking me questions the whole way?" Leo's voice was still calm, but her knuckles were turning white on top of the steering wheel.

"Maybe." Mimi kept her gaze on Leo's knuckles. It was fun to make Leo tense over just a few questions. "I've been living in London for about five years. I always wanted to go to France, especially Paris."

"Paris has too many people." Leo sounded tired. "I've been there several times, and it's never as nice as you'd think. I doubt you would like it."

"Why?" *You don't know me.* Mimi moved her gaze to Leo's face.

Leo chuckled, a sound so surprising that Mimi's own mouth twitched in a sympathy laugh before she could control herself.

"Just a guess, I doubt you would enjoy not being at the center of attention." Leo shook her head, her smile faltering and again becoming a thin line. "Maybe you can go to Paris after…." She didn't finish the sentence.

"Yeah, maybe." Mimi doubted that she'd ever return to France. Every time she heard French, a wave of nausea overcame her. She didn't think she'd ever be able to hear the language and not be transported back to *this*. Her *kidnapping*. The worst thing that had ever happened to her.

They stayed silent for a very long time. Mimi focused on the nature instead. It must have been quite early in the morning, on what day Mimi didn't know. There were few other cars on the road, and there wasn't much to look at. Only field after field. In spite of the bland surroundings, Mimi tried to take the scenery in. Leo hadn't blindfolded her, and Mimi would have been stupid to not make use of that. If she could just see something, anything. A street sign. A city name. Any landmark that she could memorize for the future. Leo's features were already burnt into her mind. Stored to be told to the police later.

"What's going to happen once we arrive?" Mimi couldn't bear the silence anymore. She wanted things to feel normal. To pretend. And to have a say in what was going to happen to her.

"We're going to lay low for a couple of days." Leo didn't look at her. "We're waiting for money to be transferred."

"From my dad."

Mimi looked at Leo, sensing the internal struggle. It was clear that she didn't know what was fine to tell her or not. It was close to being comical.

"From your dad." Leo agreed eventually. "Is money going to be a problem for him?"

Mimi shook her head.

"No, I was actually wondering why it was taking him time. He has loads of it."

Leo opened her mouth. Then closed it again. Then opened it.

"Mimi, I…," she said eventually. "I know it's not my place to ask, but if your dad is so rich, why —"

"Why do I live the way I live?" It wasn't hard to figure out what Leo was wondering. *She has been in my home after all,* Mimi reminded herself. *When she helped me home all those nights ago.* It felt like another lifetime.

"Well, yeah."

"I don't want his money." Mimi didn't have to think about her answer. "I want my own life. I may have very little, but what I have is my own. Only mine."

Leo didn't answer. She didn't even acknowledged that Mimi had answered.

"How many languages do you speak?" Mimi wasn't done talking. "I only speak English and Japanese. You seem to speak more."

"I speak English, Turkish, French, and German," Leo said it calmly, as if it was no big deal.

"How come?" *That's pretty impressive.* Mimi rolled her eyes at her own interest. She wasn't supposed to become intrigued. That wasn't the goal.

"My mother is—was—Turkish." Leo seemed to tense again. "My dad is German. I learned English in school like most people, and my boss taught me French."

"Is it your boss who wanted me kidnapped?"

"No." The word was final, but something told Mimi it wasn't. She wanted to press Leo for answers, but a rumbling in her belly beckoned her to choose other topics of conversation.

"I'm hungry." She couldn't remember the last time she had eaten.

"It's timely." Leo nodded. "There is a gas station coming up, and there as some people there I need to talk with anyway. We can buy you something to eat and drink there."

Soon they were parked outside said gas station. Mimi sat still like a good little prisoner and waited while Leo got out and walked around the car to get her. She opened and held out her hand for Mimi to take.

As soon as Mimi was standing up, Leo pulled her close and put her mouth near Mimi's ear.

"I don't have to tell you that it would be stupid for you to try anything, right?" Leo's voice was dark, hinting of danger. Her breath hot against Mimi's skin.

It made shivers travel down Mimi's spine. She wanted to pull back, but she had Leo's hand on her arm, holding her in place.

"No, ma'am," she eventually whispered.

"Good."

They walked towards the kiosk, Leo dropping her grip on Mimi's wrists as soon as they had entered.

"Go and choose whatever you want," Leo said. "But I'll have my eyes on you constantly. If you run, you won't get far."

Mimi rolled her eyes and gave an impatient nod.

Leo waved at a couple of people at the end of the kiosk.

"*Hey Didem! Buğra! Hatırladınız mı beni?*" She moved towards them, leaving Mimi alone.

Mimi watched her back for half a second, then she moved slowly toward the middle aged cashier. She tried to act as inconspicuous as possible, picked up a sandwich and a bottle of soda on the way there. She put them on the counter. Leaned forward and spoke in a low tone.

"Please." She looked pleadingly at the woman there. "I have been kidnapped. Can you help me?"

All she was met with was two big confused eyes.

"*Comment? Désolée, je ne parle pas anglais*"

"No, I need help. Help. He - e - l - p."

"*Mademoiselle, ça ne change rien même si vous parlez lentement, je ne comprends quand même pas.*"

Mimi wanted to pull on her hair in frustration, she opened her mouth to try one final time when Leo suddenly was by her side.

"C'est pour moi." Leo smiled. *"Et ça aussi."* She put another sandwich and a bottle of water next to Mimi's things. "Ready to go?"

Mimi produced what she hoped was an angelic smile and nodded.

They went back to the car once Leo had paid, bottle and sandwich in hand. Mimi was still smiling. But inside she was fuming.

Chapter Nine

Mimi didn't feel like talking for the rest of the drive. She ate her sandwich, drank her soda, and stared out of the window grumpily. She wasn't sure if Leo had caught her pathetic attempt to escape or not, but she wasn't going to ask. Mimi just wanted to forget about it.

The sun had slowly set and the gentle thrumming of the car was making her sleepy. She closed her eyes and unwillingly let the car lull her to sleep. She didn't exactly feel safe, but she was quite sure that Leo wouldn't physically hurt her.

After a dreamless nap, Mimi woke up when the car drove off the road and onto a graveled path. *Damn it.* She sat up straighter and rolled her head from side to side. She was feeling unbearably stiff, and the seat belt had cut into her neck a little bit. She yawned and stared outside the window as Leo parked the car. She couldn't believe she had fallen asleep. She had missed the road to the house. It was now dusk, and even though the white picket fence around the house was clear in the dark, there were no other landmarks visible.

The house looked dark, more than a little scary, and Mimi didn't look forward to sleeping there. There was a large tree on the right of it, a tire swing hanging from it, swinging in the evening wind in a way which only added to the spooky atmosphere

"Don't worry," Leo said as if reading Mimi's mind. "It looks better on the inside."

Mimi nodded even if she wasn't convinced.

Leo went out of the car. Stretched and yawned loudly. She went around the car and opened Mimi's door. There was no pulling, no shoving, no guns or threats. Just Leo waiting for Mimi to get out of the car of her own free will.

"I'm hungry." Mimi felt a bit embarrassed as she got out the car, her stomach already growling.

But Leo just chuckled softly.

"Of course you are. I've got some things. I'll cook."

Leo did take a hold of her arm as they walked toward the house, but the hold wasn't very hard, and she wasn't pulling Mimi along. They simply walked together up to the house.

When they got inside, Leo let go of her and turned the light on.

"I'll make some food and then we'll find a bed, okay?"

"Okay." Mimi was looking forward to a warm meal. And eating by a table and not while lying down.

She was eager to eat. Then sleep. It didn't matter that Mimi had just napped for hours. She felt so tired. And she needed more rest if she was going to manage to run away in the morning. Leo had been warming up to her, that much was clear. Soon she'd slip up and Mimi would only need one chance. She was ready. Then her stupid dad could keep his stupid money. And Mimi could go back to her own life.

In spite of Leo's promises that the house would "look better on the inside," it really didn't. It looked like a traditional French farmhouse, lime plaster walls, wooden beams in the ceiling, wooden furniture. Maybe it looked idyllic in the light of day, to Mimi it just looked cold.

They walked to the kitchen, and Leo put a bag on the counter, next to the stove. She turned on the light and gave Mimi a look.

"I won't go anywhere." Mimi sat down on a chair. The kitchen was fully furnished even though the stove and fridge looked old. The chair was wooden and cold against her back. "You don't need to tell me."

"Good." Leo turned to her bag.

Mimi smiled towards Leo's back. Leo was starting to trust her, slowly. *Perfect.*

She regarded Leo cooking, and soon the scent of sausage and fried potato filled the kitchen. It made Mimi's mouth water despite it not being her favorite type of food. When a plate was placed in front of her, Mimi dug in.

*

"Do you have to handcuff me?" Leo had chosen a bedroom for them at random, and they were standing by a large bed, looking at it. Leo looked down at her.

"Please," Mimi continued. "I just want a good night's sleep."

She could see that Leo was thinking hard, and she tried to look as cute and innocent as possible. She batted her eyelashes, but then a big yawn overtook her. It wasn't a lie, she really was tired. She wanted to curl up and sleep. *Stupid drugs.* Once she was back home, she needed to go to a doctor to make sure there were no lasting medical effects.

"I have to, I'm sorry." Leo pointed at the bed and waited until Mimi lay down.

Mimi stared at her hatefully while she was again handcuffed with one hand to the bed. Luckily the chain was longer than the other one, and she could most likely sleep comfortably. *Maybe I can still get free during the night somehow, I can—*

"What are you doing?"

Her blood ran cold when Leo lay down next to her. The bed was large, and no part of their bodies touched, but if Leo was next to her all night Mimi wouldn't manage to escape.

"I'm not leaving you alone in here." Leo turned off the light next to the bed. "This is just how it will have to be."

Mimi pursed her lip, but in the darkness no one could see her scowl.

"Well, goodnight then."

Mimi refused to answer. She closed her eyes and willed sleep to come quickly.

*

It was the thunder that woke her up. Branches were beating against the window and wind made the old wood rattle. She whimpered in the darkness, unsure of where she was and what had happened. She kicked the sweaty blanket off and whined again when lightening lit up the room. She struck out with her arms and met something solid behind her. Without really thinking, Mimi did the only thing that felt normal. She took hold of the arm she felt there and pulled it protectively around her own body. The body next to her grumbled something in a language that Mimi didn't recognize but then pulled her closer. Cradled against a soft chest, Mimi felt safe again. She smiled in the dark and went right back to sleep.

Chapter Ten

Leo woke up with goosebumps on her flesh. Her night had been filled with strange dreams, and she was relieved to be awake. From her position, it looked like the beginning of a beautiful day, she could see the blue sky through the window, and if she focused, she could hear bird song in the distance. Leo hugged the body in her arms tighter. Cuddling after a dream like that was perfect, just what she needed. The warm and female body in her arms snuggled back in her embrace, and Leo hummed contently. For a moment everything was perfect. Then the cold metal of a chain touched her bare arm.

Wait a minute. Leo opened her eyes and stared into Mimi surprised face. They stared at each other in panic. *How the fuck did this happen?* Leo's heart beat like a captive bird, and sweat trickled down her spine. She tried to think of something to say. Anything. Anything to stop the panic coursing through her veins.

"Sorry, I was sleeping," Leo eventually mumbled and rolled away from Mimi.

Mimi looked absolutely panicked, which made Leo want to punch herself. This was already a scary and stressful time for her, and Leo hated the thought that she had added to it. Cuddling had definitely not been on her mind when she had decided for them to sleep in the same bed. She felt her face flush and the need to run away became overwhelming.

"I'm really sorry." Leo wanted to make Mimi believe the sincerity of her words. "I never meant to scare you." She wanted to apologize overtly for snuggling during the night but couldn't bring the words to pass her lips. She regarded Mimi in silence.

Mimi breathed in deeply.

"It's okay." Her words were small. She kept her gaze on the mattress. "I think I started hugging you in the night. There was thunder." Her cheeks reddened at the admission, and she looked so embarrassed.

Leo swallowed, her throat dry all of a sudden. It was Mimi who had reached for her? Leo's heart broke all over again. Proud Mimi. Hurt, angry Mimi. How scared she must have been to reach for her during the night.

Leo decided to drop it right away. There was no need to make things weirder between them.

"Do you want some breakfast?"

As if on cue, Mimi's eyes lit up a bit. She smiled. "Yes, please."

*

All they had were the sausages from last night, and when Leo put a plate in front of Mimi, she did not look nearly as happy as she had last night.

"Do we have nothing else?" She had a sullen face as she cut the sausage into smaller pieces, looking like a petulant child.

"Afraid not." The sausages she had placed in front of Mimi were all they had, and Leo sat down with just a glass of water. She wished they had had coffee or tea. The big house was minimally heated, and once out of bed, Leo really needed something else to warm her up.

"Can we go and buy food?" Mimi's question was almost expected.

Leo nodded.

"We don't have much choice. We don't have any more."

"And if you're going to keep me prisoner you might as well keep me fed." Mimi shoved several pieces of sausage into her mouth.

Leo had to stop herself from laughing, she had never met anyone who loved food as much as Mimi did.

She drank her water while Mimi finished her plate. She then got up to do the dishes.

"I want to change my clothes today." Mimi said behind her. "I've been wearing these for…."

Mimi fell silent for a moment, then she sobbed loudly.

"Why are you crying?" Leo turned around.

Mimi looked up at her with tear-filled eyes.

"I can't remember how many days it's been." She brought up her hands and fisted her hair as if planning to pull it out in frustration. "Why did you do this to me? I can't… I can't remember."

"It's been four days." Leo said calmly. "No more than that."

"Why does it feel like longer?" If Mimi was still looking at her, Leo didn't know, because she had resumed doing the dishes.

Angry Mimi she could handle, Mimi the escapist she could handle, Mimi the pain-in-the-ass she could handle. But Leo had no idea what to do with sad Mimi.

She finished the dishes and sat back down by the table. Mimi was still crying, loud sobs that made her whole body jump, her face hidden in the palms of her hands.

Leo still didn't know what to do. She wasn't good with crying people under normal circumstances. There was nothing she could do. No hugging, no 'there, there.' All she could do was wait until Mimi finished on her own.

Which Mimi eventually did. Her sobbing subsided and she wiped her wet face with the front of her shirt.

Leo's phone beeped. She put her back toward Mimi and looked at it. It was Sandra, with instructions.

"I'm supposed to call your dad now." Leo felt strangely empty. "We need to call him to prove that we have you and that you're alive."

"I don't want to talk with him." Mimi's voice was gravely. "Take a photo."

She took a step back and stared forward. She was waiting for Leo to take a photo, that much was clear. But Leo didn't want to. Mimi's expression was empty, her hair dirty, her cheeks red whilst the rest of her face was pale. Her lips pale. Her eyes filled with misery. Leo couldn't help but compare it to a few days ago.

She hesitated. But what could she say? What argument could she give? She went over to a sideboard, took out a piece of paper, and wrote today's date on it. She then gave it for Mimi to hold while she took the photo.

Smile. The sarcastic word was there, it would have been so easy for Leo to say it. Slip back into the role of cruel kidnapper. But she couldn't.

When she sent the text to Mimi's dad, she waited. Sandra had told her to call and then throw the phone away. What was she supposed to do? To her distress, Leo realized that she had gone against Sandra's instructions. She couldn't remember ever doing that before. She hadn't done what Sandra had told her to do, simply because Mimi didn't want to talk with her dad. *You have spent too much time with Mimi now,* Leo thought to herself, *this must be some kind of reverse Stockholm-syndrome.*

The phone called. They both stared at it.

"Shouldn't you pick up?" Mimi asked her.

"I don't want to." Leo really didn't want to. She didn't want to face Mimi's dad, not even over the phone. And if Sandra wanted to talk with her, surely she would use Leo's own phone? Leo didn't recognize the number.

"What were you supposed to do after calling him?"

The phone kept ringing.

"Throw the phone away."

"So, let's."

"What?" Mimi's actions made no sense. "Don't you want to talk with your dad?"

"I'm not into trading one jailor for the other." She shrugged. "Throw the phone away. I want to wash my face." She folded her arms over her chest and looked questioningly at Leo.

Leo felt frozen in the spot. She couldn't process what was going on. Maybe she was the one who had been drugged this time. She blinked once. Eventually she put the phone on the table, she would decide what to do with it later.

"Of course."

They walked upstairs to the large bathroom that was there, and she let Mimi go in by herself. At least she could have some privacy there. There was no window in there anyway. Perfectly safe. She waited patiently at first, leaned up against the door.

"Mimi?" Eventually she had to check, having heard no noises at all for a little while.

"Just give me a minute." Mimi's tone was equally sad and angry. "It's the least you can do, don't you fucking think?"

Leo didn't reply, instead she let her legs give out and she slid down until she sat with her back against the door. As long as Mimi wasn't hurting herself, Leo didn't mind waiting for her.

When Mimi finally opened the bathroom door, her tears were gone. Leo got up.

"I'm sorry for breaking down like that." Her voice was void of any emotion and she didn't meet Leo's gaze. "I want to take a shower now. And I want to put on clean clothes when I get out."

It was perfectly understandable. Mimi hadn't changed clothes since Leo had kidnapped her, and for a woman who loved fashion as much as Mimi did, it must have been hell.

"I have some clothes that you can borrow."

Mimi snorted.

"I doubt we have the same style. Or size," she said, some of the usual fire back in her voice. "But it'll be good enough for now. And when I've showered, you're going to bring my sewing machine and the fabrics I have."

"Huh?"

"I'm bored." Mimi looked at her now. "Even if this house has a library hidden away somewhere, the books are probably all in French." Leo still didn't answer so Mimi continued, mockery in her voice. "I'm bored, oh great kidnapper, I need to do something otherwise all you'll deliver to my dad in a couple of days is a neurotic mess."

"I'll see what I can do."

"It's not rocket science." Mimi rolled her eyes. "It's all out there in the car. Just go and get it. Lock me in the bathroom with a towel and I'll take a shower while you get it."

Leo didn't know what to answer. She understood that Mimi's attempts at ordering her around was a way to get back some resemblance of control, and Leo didn't mind. But she couldn't let go of the feeling that Mimi was trying to trick her somehow.

Luckily the bathroom was an old one, with normal lock and key. It would be easy for Leo to use the key to lock it on the outside with Mimi inside.

"Okay, we can do that."

She took a hold of Mimi's arm to reestablish some of her authority, and they walked back into the room where they had slept and also kept the bag with Leo's gun and other belongings. She took out a pair of shorts, a pair of panties, and a T-shirt that said '*Hope is a dangerous thing.*' After a moment of hesitation, she put the shirt back and exchanged it for one with no motif. She also went through Sandra's cabinets until she found a big fluffy towel. She then handed them all to Mimi.

"I don't have any soap or shampoo. If you're lucky, there will be some in the shower." Leo added it to her mental shopping list. She'd want to take a shower later too, somehow.

They walked together back to the bathroom, Mimi in the front, and Leo keeping close behind her.

They didn't look at each other as Mimi went inside the bathroom and Leo locked the door. Pocketed the key.

As if on autopilot, she went downstairs and headed out to the car. She grabbed Mimi's boxes and closed the car door with her foot. Even though she had carried them twice before, she was again struck by how heavy they were. It must be quite the workout for Mimi to carry them around day after day. Maybe even bad for her back.

Leo shook her head, annoyed with herself. She had to stop thinking about Mimi. This was supposed to be a break for her. Mimi was locked in and couldn't get into trouble. This was supposed to be Leo's reprieve when she could think of other things, maybe call some friends, plan for the weekend. She laughed mirthlessly at no one. There were no friends to call. No weekend to plan for. Her job was her life. It was pathetic that it had taken a kidnapping for her to realize that.

The money better be transferred soon, Leo thought as she hurried up to the house. *I need to get rid of Mimi before I lose my mind.*

Chapter Eleven

Mimi was falling in love with the bathroom. She was starting to like the faint smell of mildew, the stained sink, and the tacky flower-patterned shower drapes. *I could make this my home,* she thought and wondered if maybe Leo would let her sleep in there. The floor wouldn't be comfortable, but it was better to risk back pain than wake up in Leo's arms again. *Fucking Leo.* Mimi could vaguely remember putting her arms around Leo in the night now, but it was still the other woman's fault. Somehow.

Mimi sighed and looked at the mirror above the sink. She didn't recognize the woman in it. Even her lips looked pale. She looked at the bathroom floor. No, she didn't want to sleep there. The bathroom wasn't better than what was on the other side. The bathroom didn't mean freedom. At best it was a cage of protection.

Mimi decided to think positively. Soon she would be clean, in clean clothes, and working on something new on the sewing machine. If Leo could also produce a nice meal for lunch, Mimi would consider this a good day. She had to. It was that or madness.

She took her clothes off and let them lie on the floor. *A good day.* She couldn't believe she had actually thought those words. She had been kidnapped, stuffed in a trunk, tied up, gagged, and drugged. All by Leo. As long as Mimi was close to Leo, there would be no such thing as a good day.

Done admonishing herself, she pulled back the shower curtain and frowned in disappointment. All there was was a bottle of men's combination shampoo and soap. She opened it and smelled it. *Well,* she thought, *at this point I rather smell like a man and be clean than the alternative.* She would ask Leo for a better soap.

She started the water and got in. As the warm rays of water hit her, Mimi did smile and almost moaned. This was bliss. When she took up the bottle of "sport scented" soap, poured a generous amount in her hand, and started lathering her body, she no longer cared about the smell. Nothing could ruin the sensation of getting clean. Absolutely nothing. Even if she winced as she accidently touched a scrape or a bruise, the water and soap soothed her tired body and exhausted soul.

She heard steps outside the door, and even if she wanted to drag it out, make Leo wait, she also wanted to sit down and play with her sewing machine. It would make her feel normal. Even more normal than the shower had.

She rinsed the rest of the soap off, washed her hair quickly, and turned the water off. As she started drying herself with the fluffy towel that Leo had handed her before, Mimi regarded the drawers under the sink. For one moment she played with the thought of opening them, finding a sharp nail file, a pair of scissors or —

No. Mimi shook her head. Even if she could find it in herself to stick something sharp in Leo's neck, what then? She was in the middle of nowhere, no phone, nor any idea where the nearest town was. She was stuck. It was better to wait for the right time to run away. She also had to admit to herself that sticking something sharp in Leo's neck didn't appeal to her at all.

She rinsed the rest of the soap off, washed her hair and then she turned the water off. She wasn't scared anymore. She was annoyed, angry, still wanted to run away, but she was no longer afraid. She just didn't think that Leo would hurt her. Stop her from running away, probably, maybe tie her up again, but Mimi also knew that Leo wouldn't do anything to intentionally hurt her.

When she was dry she looked through the small pile of clothes that Leo had handed her earlier. Even panties. *Good,* Mimi thought, *I had forgotten about underwear.* As she pulled the T-shirt over her narrow shoulders, she couldn't help but notice how it smelled like Leo. She pulled it to her nose and inhaled deeply, the scent causing butterflies to flit around her stomach. She dropped it like she'd been burnt.

"Definitely time to get a grip," she said to herself. She pulled the shorts up and tied the towel around her head. She hoped that Leo would have a brush, she had forgotten to ask about that.

There was a knock on the door.

"Are you dressed?"

Mimi looked down at the plain T-shirt and the shorts. She would hardly call it *dressed* but….

"Yes." At least she was clean.

The door creaked when Leo unlocked and opened it.

"I'm going to order some groceries online, and then we can drive and pick them up in an hour."

Mimi nodded mindlessly, she just wanted to go downstairs and sew something. But first she needed to fix the wet mess on the top of her head.

"Do you have a brush?"

"Huh?" Leo stared as Mimi pointed to the wet, messy hair on top of her head. "Yeah, I do."

Out of Hand

After Mimi had brushed her hair and returned the wet towel to the bathroom, they walked downstairs together. Mimi tried not to skip with joy when she saw the box with her sewing machine on the table in the kitchen. She ran over to it and started unpacking it right away.

"Do you have an adaptor?" Mimi held out the cable toward Leo, who was watching her from the door.

"Fuck." Leo took the cable in her hand and inspected the plug. "I don't have one like this."

Mimi swallowed back tears.

"So no sewing?" She hadn't known that she had been looking forward to it that much. She needed it. Something from her own reality. Something to focus on. The idea that she wouldn't get to sew was like a punch to the gut.

"You will." Leo gave her back the cable. "I will get you an adaptor from somewhere."

Mimi didn't believe her. She felt like Christmas had been cancelled and nothing Leo said could make her feel better.

"I'll place an order for the supermarket." Leo took out her phone. "What do you feel like eating?"

*

"How handy," Mimi said as Leo started the car. "For kidnappers, I mean. Getting groceries without letting your prisoner out of your sight."

Leo didn't reply, seemingly occupied with looking at the road ahead and adjusting the mirrors *again.* If Mimi didn't know better she would have thought that Leo was ignoring her. Mimi, however, was in a good mood again. They were going to get not just food, but an adaptor and some more black thread. Leo had placed an order, and all they had to do was pick up the already packed groceries.

"Why am I not blindfolded?"

"What?" Leo turned her head quickly to look at Mimi then back at the road.

"Why am I not blindfolded?" She repeated. "I know your face. I know that man we stayed with before. I could identify the two of you in a line-up. And now I know the place we're staying at is near Strasbourg. It just doesn't seem very smart."

"Do you wish you were blindfolded?" Leo sounded tired.

"Of course not," Mimi said. "I'm just thinking out loud." She grinned. "If I had to fill in a guest comment card, I'd give you ten for effort but about two for poor execution."

"I'm not a planner." Leo sighed. "And I've never kidnapped someone before. My boss didn't give me enough time to think this through."

"I'm going to name you." Mimi smiled widely. "Leo. Leo-something, tall, dark hair. You better hope you're out of the country once my dad calls the police. Actually, you better hope to be out of Europe."

Leo gripped the steering wheel a bit harder, and her jaw tensed. Mimi wanted to laugh out loud.

"Will you tell me the name of your boss? Make it a bit easier for me?"

Bothering Leo was just too much fun. Mimi opened her mouth again to say something else.

"Don't." Leo was faster. "If you want your adaptor, your thread, and your fucking baguette you will shut up right now."

Mimi closed her mouth. As fun as threatening and teasing Leo was, she really did want that baguette. And she needed the adaptor.

"Fine," she said grumpily and turned to look out of the window.

They didn't talk for the rest of the drive. Mimi had nothing more to say anyway, she was planning her escape.

Chapter Twelve

"You better be quiet now, okay?" Leo didn't trust her, not Mimi's nod, not her angelic smile. "If you create any kind of trouble you won't get any food."

Pathetic. Leo once again wished that she had never accepted this tedious and difficult mission. She had no leverage. She was quite sure that Mimi knew Leo didn't want to hurt her, and because of this she had no threats to give out. She just wasn't sure that food was enough incentive for Mimi to behave well until they drove back to the house.

They were just a few blocks from the supermarket now, and Leo still didn't know how she was going to both get the food and keep Mimi with her. She couldn't walk around the store with a gun to Mimi's head and she didn't have anything to drug her with. And even if she had had something to drug her with, Leo had to admit that she didn't want to drug Mimi again. If she placed her in the trunk she would make a lot of noise. Leo didn't know what to do.

"What are you doing?" Mimi asked when Leo circled the same block for the third time.

Leo didn't answer, reluctant to admit that she was feeling unsure.

"You could just let me go, you know?" Mimi's tone was mischievous. "All of this can end if you want it. I'll be out of your hair. I won't say your name. I'll only mention the man who hit me. What was his name?"

"Be quiet."

Leo didn't have much choice, she needed to call in a favor.

*

Mimi looked on as Leo took out her phone and dialed a number. She had noticed the inner conflict and had hoped for a moment that Leo would set her free.

But now the stone cold surety was back in Leo's eyes, and she was clicking on her phone. She put it against her ear. And again, to Mimi's annoyance, spoke in a language she didn't understand.

"*Aylin? Merhaba ben Leo. Yardimina ihtiyacim var. Tamam, yeri gelince geri öderim.*" She kept talking for a little while, sounding more and more agitated. "Fine," she eventually muttered in English and turned it off. As soon as she put her phone away, she fell forward and leaned her head on top of her hands on the steering wheel.

"What is it?" Mimi couldn't help but asking.

"An acquaintance is getting us the stuff. She wanted me to do something for her in return. A favor for a favor." Leo kept her head down.

"Is she a kidnapper too?" Mimi asked within a heartbeat. "Coworker of yours?"

"Not telling." Leo was resting her mouth against the top of her hands now and the words came out muffled.

"So tell me something else. Why can't you just let me go? You clearly don't like me. But you also don't want to hurt me. Do you even have your gun with you? Do you have anything to drug me with?"

Leo lifted her head and gave her a look that told Mimi everything she needed to know. Leo really hadn't brought drugs or her gun.

"I don't get you," Mimi said. "I really don't get you. Just let me go, okay? I won't give your name, I promise." In that moment, Mimi meant it. She would leave Leo out of it. Say she hadn't seen her face, not heard her name, not noticed anything. She wanted to soothe the desperate look in Leo's eyes. She wanted to reach over and take Leo's hand, she was grabbing the steering wheel so hard again, but Mimi stopped herself.

"Why does owing a favor scare you so much?" She asked instead, putting her hands under her thighs to keep them in place.

"Ever had that older bully cousin who always asks you to do vile things you don't want to do?"

"Was that your cousin?"

Leo shook her head but didn't say anything.

"No, I haven't," Mimi said. "I was the family's little princess growing up. No one would dare to hurt me." It wasn't necessarily the truth, but Mimi didn't care. It suited her image. "What did the person on the phone ask you to do?"

"Deliver something." Leo groaned. "You should stop asking me questions."

"No." Mimi couldn't help smiling. "But you should probably stop answering them. I thought you had no scruples. What doesn't the evil kidnapper Leo want to deliver? What is beneath even her?"

Leo laughed mirthlessly.

"Shocker, I know," she says. "But I'm not completely without morals."

"You *kidnapped* me. You've transported me over borders. You have drugged me." Mimi's list was longer but she stopped there. "A moral person doesn't do any of those things."

"Can't really argue with that," Leo muttered.

"So why don't you let me go?" The once rhetorical question was now asked sincerely.

"Because." Leo sucked in air through her mouth. "I owe it to my boss."

"I don't care what she has done for you, this isn't okay."

"I know that." Leo sounded agitated. "But if I didn't agree to do it, she was going to send somebody else to take you and I thought you'd be safer with me. I know you don't think I care, but at least with me you won't be raped, beaten, or drugged beyond repair. My boss gave me an opportunity to get out, and I didn't take it. So I do owe it to her to see this through." She fell silent, breathing deeply.

Mimi stared at her. She had no answers to give. In spite of what Leo had said, Mimi could feel no gratitude, and she didn't think Leo expected that either. One thing that she did realize though, was that Leo did care. Maybe not about Mimi as a person, but at least as an expensive stolen painting needing to be kept whole until returned to her rightful owner. Mimi felt a surge of anger rise within her. She wasn't a painting. She was a person. And she hated every person who had reduced her to less. She regarded the back of Leo's head. For some reason her hatred did not encompass the woman next to her. Mimi didn't dare to think about why.

They waited the rest of the time in silence and peace since Mimi saw no reason to attempt escape. The car was parked in a dark alley and there were no people to wave too. The door was locked and she had no way to physically overthrow Leo. So she sat silently, feeling a little bit bored and restless.

After a very long time, Mimi didn't know how long, there was a quick knock on the back of the car. Leo looked into the rearview mirror.

"Good," she mumbled as if to herself.

Mimi looked into the mirror but couldn't see anything, it was as if Leo's acquaintance knew exactly where to stay so Mimi wouldn't see her.

Their trunk was opened and then closed, and somebody knocked on the lid.

Mimi turned around in her seat, wanting to see the mysterious person who had come out of nowhere to get their food. She didn't see a face but a black hoodie and blue jeans.

"Did she get my adaptor?" She sat down properly in her seat when Leo started the car.

"I told her to." Leo sounded tired. "I also told her to get some coconut-scented shampoo."

"Thank you."

Mimi had nothing more to say, it felt as if the air had gone out of her. She didn't even grieve her missed chance of escape, she just felt confused as the humming of the engine once more lulled her to sleep.

*

When she woke up they were back at the house. *I've never slept this much before.* Maybe it was a residual effect from the drugs.

"Before we eat I want to take a shower." Leo said as she turned off the car and unlocked the door. She got out and went around the car, but before she had reached Mimi's side, Mimi had opened the door herself and got out. Mimi almost expected Leo to get angry with her, but she just nodded in silence. Their gazes met. Leo looked utterly exhausted and a little bit lost. It was so clear that she didn't like this situation, that keeping Mimi made her uncomfortable.

Mimi was about to open her mouth and again try to convince Leo to let her go. She didn't manage before Leo averted her gaze, grabbed Mimi's arm, and held it in a harder grip than she had for a very long time. She held on as they went to the trunk of the car and got a bag from there. With groceries in one hand and Mimi in the other, Leo led them toward the house with quick steps.

Her grip was turning painful and Mimi winced.

"You're hurting me." Mimi tried to pull her arm free, but Leo wasn't listening.

She didn't let go until they were both inside and the door behind them was locked.

"I'm sorry for hurting you." Leo didn't look at Mimi but gestured for her to walk in front of Leo into the kitchen. "I can't let you get away. You have to understand that."

She put the bag on the counter and started unpacking it. Mimi sat down by the table and put her chin in her hands.

"I don't have to understand anything."

"I'm just following orders." Leo sounded distraught, which infuriated Mimi. *Damn her for making me feel guilty.* She did feel sorry for Leo, as pathetic as it was.

"I don't care if you're following orders," she said. "I don't remember anyone holding a gun to your head as you drove us out of London. Nobody forced you to put me in the trunk. You had a choice. The one without choices here is me."

Mimi swallowed back more harsh words that were tickling the back of her throat. She didn't want to lose her patience, didn't want to give in to the fury that was boiling in her blood. Instead she got up, her movements erratic and jumpy. She pulled the bag of root vegetables from Leo's hand, got a knife and a cutting board, and started slicing them.

"Get me a pan and some oil and spices," she commanded.

In silence, Leo did as she was told.

Soon, the vegetables were roasting in the oven. Mimi stood next to the oven, temporarily unable to move. She wanted to be free again, she wanted to run and sew and be grateful for her stupid little life that at least was completely her own.

"I'm sorry." Leo's words were soft and so unexpected that Mimi first thought she had imagined them.

She turned around and looked at Leo with her arms crossed over her chest.

"I have all the power here," Leo continued. "You're a pain in the ass, don't get me wrong. But I'm the one who has a choice. Not you."

Mimi observed her silently. Eventually she nodded.

"Thank you." She pulled a breath in through her nose. "Why did you?"

Leo gestured for her to follow and they went through the hallway and up the stairs.

"Why did I do what?" She asked when they stopped by the room they slept in to pick up a chance of clothes for Leo and a towel.

"Why did you fucking kidnap me?" Mimi wasn't angry, just impatient.

Leo said nothing as they went into the bathroom and Leo locked the door. She kept the key in her hand while she went closer to the shower. All of a sudden she started taking her clothes off. Mimi's eyes went wide and all words escaped her. For a tenth of a second, Mimi forgot that Leo was indeed her kidnapper and not at all absolutely gorgeous. Tall and lean, with subtle muscles under pale olive skin. Mimi swallowed, her mouth dry as her gaze went first higher and then lower and fixated upon—

Leo coughed and Mimi forced her gaze upwards. Leo was looking at her with a disturbed, and slightly amused, look in her eyes. She didn't seem ashamed by her nudity, but Mimi felt her face heat up and she turned around.

"Well?" She hurried to change subject, her back still to Leo. "What do you have to say for yourself? Why did you kidnap me?"

The shower was started behind her.

"I have said it before," Leo said. "I've worked for my boss a long time. She's not a woman you can say no to."

"That doesn't tell me anything." She was annoyed with Leo, and she was annoyed with herself. She wanted a proper answer, and she knew she wouldn't get one. She needed to understand. She wanted to make sense of what had happened.

She listened to a shampoo bottle being opened and the sweeping noises of fingers on wet skin. The more Mimi listened, the angrier she got. It really wasn't appropriate for her to get to listen to Leo taking a shower. It wasn't her fault that her head filled with images of what was going on behind her. She wasn't the one in charge, she wasn't the one with a choice, it was Leo's fault. Everything was Leo's fault.

Mimi forced her eyes closed and grabbed the sink, holding herself in place. She wouldn't let herself turn around and feast her eyes on the one person in the world that she really should have hated but for some reason couldn't. She didn't turn around until Leo was done and dressed.

*

Once they had finished eating, Leo suggested they take a walk outside. They had eaten in complete silence, and with her belly full of food, she didn't feel like walking around the premises. But curiosity won over laziness and she agreed.

The sun was shining outside, peeking through the foliage. The house was located on top of a field, shielded from the rest of the world by birches and oak trees. The ground was hard, as if frozen underneath, but spring flowers stood around the roots of the trees, seemingly huddled together for warmth. Mimi put her arms around herself, shivered.

"Would she have killed you if you had refused?" It was too silent, in spite of the bird song. "Your boss, I mean." She couldn't let go of the topic. She *needed* to understand.

"I don't think so." Leo had her back to Mimi. *Did she not think that I would run away?* It made Mimi want to try.

"Then you didn't have to."

"I supposed I didn't."

Mimi didn't know what to say after that. She didn't know what she was after, what she wanted to do. What it was that she wanted to accomplish.

"Whatever." She leaned against a tree, the solidness of it giving her comfort.

"What about you?" Leo came and leaned her back against the same thick tree. "Where are you from? Your dad lives here right? *Sprichst du deutsch?*"

Mimi knew enough about languages to be able to guess that Leo had asked her if she spoke German. She shook her head, kicked back against the tree.

"My dad is German by birth, but we lived in the states for most of my life. We spoke English with him or Japanese with Mom. They only moved to Germany when I was nineteen and then I didn't want to go with them."

"So you moved to London instead."

"Yes, I've always loved London." Mimi took a few steps into the woods, she could hear Leo following behind her. Wind came between the trees, pulling at her hair and making her shiver. Dark clouds were gathering above them. "I think it's going to rain."

"We don't need to go inside," Leo said. "If you rather stay outside." Her words finished with a distant rumbling of thunder.

"Why are you being nice?"

"It's the least I can do."

Mimi snorted but didn't answer at first. But when the first drops fell and landed on her naked arm, she asked to go inside anyway. At least her house-shaped cage was warm and dry.

When they got inside, Leo started doing the dishes from their lunch. She acted casual, as if she wouldn't chase her if Mimi tried to run away. It was a beautiful illusion. As if they were friends, on a weekend trip in France.

Mimi sighed. Said nothing. She sat down by the wooden table in the kitchen, grabbed the lined legal pad that laid there, and started sketching on an idea for the dress she wanted to make. Since she didn't have any buttons or a zipper, she'd have to make it out of the stretchiest fabric she had. When she finished the sketch, she got some fabric and other things she needed out of her boxes and started working on it.

Outside thunder was rumbling loudly now, and lightening lit up the kitchen. Mimi twitched involuntarily. She wasn't scared, but thunder made her uncomfortable. She focused harder on the fabric in front of her, cutting it and stitching it together. As the rain started pouring down outside, Mimi plugged in her sewing machine and finally started to put her dress together. Leo had, in the meantime, got a book out and sat down in front of her, reading while she worked.

"There," Mimi announced and held out the dress.

"Wow." Leo leaned over to finger the fabric. "That's actually quite impressive."

Mimi couldn't help but be flattered. The dress she had made was a simple, blue, A-line dress with no flair or ornaments. It was almost funny how impressed Leo looked by it.

"Thanks," she said. "Can't wait to put it on."

Without caring about Leo's gaze, Mimi pulled the shorts and T-shirt off, and pulled the dress over her head right there in the kitchen. She didn't care if Leo ogled her, and she didn't think that she would.

The dress was a little bit looser than she'd wanted, she'd lost a little bit of baby fat during her time in France, but otherwise it fit perfectly. She ran her hands over her hips.

"Where did you learn how to make clothes?" Leo had put the book down and was watching Mimi run her hands down the length of the short skirt.

"My nanny taught me." Mimi smiled, "I was bored one day, and she taught me to keep me from whining. My mother didn't like it though. Thought it was servant work." She gritted her teeth and clutched a handful of fabric. "I love sewing. It's the best skill for a fashion lover, I wish my mother could have seen that."

"It doesn't bring in much money though, does it?" Leo looked so genuinely curious that Mimi forgot to be annoyed.

"No," she said. "Most people go to Primark, Topshop, or even H&M. There isn't a lot of room for a seamstress trying to make it in this day and age. At least not in London."

"It's a job of the past."

Mimi snorted.

"Well, at least I'm not a… whatever you are." She pulled the plug out of the wall and put her sewing machine back into the box.

"I'm a smuggler." Leo grinned. *Is she proud?* Mimi shook her head in disapproval.

"Talk about a job from the past."

"Yeah." Leo chuckled and Mimi felt the tips of mouth begging to move upwards. "I don't really have an answer for that."

Mimi sank back down on the chair and sighed.

"What now?" She leaned forward and rested her chin in her hands, fixing her gaze on Leo's face. "I'm bored."

"Do you want to watch a movie?" Leo sounded unsure.

They looked at each other in silence. Eventually Mimi nodded.

"I suppose we might as well. It's not like you're going to drive me back to London, even if I ask nicely."

Chapter Thirteen

"Can we have breakfast now? I always wake up hungry."

Leo couldn't help but chuckle. Mimi and herself could not be more different when it came to food.

"Good morning to you too."

Mimi held out her hand, and Leo's smile disappeared. She sighed as she undid the handcuff that was wrapped around Mimi's left arm.

"Come on." Leo got up and rubbed her face with her palms. "Let's brush our teeth and then go about getting you that breakfast."

They went to the bathroom, and then headed down to the kitchen. Mimi looked grumpy.

She's so cute when she's in a bad mood, Leo thought. *Like an angry kitten.*

"Should I make some coffee?" She offered.

"If you want," Mimi muttered while she took out some vegetables and started cutting them. It was only when she had finished cutting one of the potatoes that Leo realized that perhaps giving her captive a knife wasn't the best idea. Not that Mimi seemed to reflect on the fact that she'd been given a weapon not just once, but twice now. Her mind seemed to be focused on cooking and not escaping. For once.

"Do you like cooking a lot?" Leo had to ask. Mimi didn't come off as the most domestic type.

"Not when it's just for me." Mimi kept her eyes on the cutting board. "And it's been a while since I cooked for someone else."

"You don't have a boyfriend... or a girlfriend?" Leo wasn't sure which way Mimi swung, but whatever she was, Leo refused to believe that a woman like Mimi could be single for a long period of time. Bitchiness aside, Mimi was gorgeous, and no doubt had lots of suitors from both genders. Especially people with a taste for high maintenance women.

"Oh, I've had plenty." Mimi laughed. "Rich, powerful men my dad thought were good enough. And lots of men my dad didn't think were good enough." She looked thoughtful for a moment. In front of her, a tortilla was cooking away. "If I had dared, I would have told him about the women as well." She shook her head. "But no one has wanted me to cook for them anyway. I guess I don't look the type." She held out her hand until Leo handed her two plates, then she plated the food.

They sat down to eat, which was done quickly. Neither of them spoke.

"So you're a dyke?" Mimi asked and licked the remnants of food from her fork.

"What?" Leo's mouth dropped open. "I mean, it's generally not the term I'd use but... Why would you say that?" *How does she know?*

"Just a feeling I get." Mimi shrugged. "Have you always liked girls?" She put their plates together and pushed them to the middle of the table.

"Why are you asking?" Leo didn't mind talking about it, but she wondered why Mimi was curious.

"During my youth the only times any of my friends went for other girls, it was to get back at their parents. As soon as they were satisfied they always went back to men."

Leo couldn't stop her face from making a disgusted grimace.

"What about the women they stayed with?" She asked. "Did they find other bored straight girls?"

"I don't know." Mimi's eyes widened at Leo's dark tone. "What is it? Are you angry?"

Leo rolled her eyes and leaned backwards, cup in hand. *Straight girls are all the same.*

"Why did you get angry?" Mimi seemed honestly baffled, and the gentle look in her eyes even showed concern.

"Let's just do the dishes." Leo got up and grabbed their plates, no longer in the mood to talk. She went to the sink and started filling it with hot water.

"I might be a criminal," she said after a little while. "And I live on the margins of society. I don't belong to any clubs. I don't have a hometown. I don't even consider any country my own. I have no family. What I do have is the LGBT community, whether they want me or not. As stereotypical as it might sound, I'm proud to be gay. So the thought of a group of spoiled and bored little rich girls taking advantage of—"

"I can stop your little monologue right there." Mimi held up her hand. "Maybe some of those girls were bisex—"

"Does it matter?" It was Leo's turn to interrupt. "They still left a string of broken hearts behind, and for what?"

Mimi laughed out loud.

"Broken hearts! My kidnapper, ladies and gentlemen, concerned with broken hearts!"

Leo grimaced and turned toward the dishes again.

"Did you do the same?" She had to ask. "Did you date women to hurt your parents?"

At this question Mimi was quiet for such a long time that Leo had to check that she was still there. Mimi's face looked sad, and a mixed set of emotions ran across her face. She opened her mouth as if to say something, but nothing came out.

"What?" Leo asked. "What is it?"

"I didn't date as a form of rebellion." Mimi leaned back in the chair, keeping her gaze to the side. "Not women at least." Her voice had gone very soft, and when she inhaled it sounded like she was about to start crying. Leo wanted to ask but didn't. Whatever memories Mimi was remembering, it wasn't Leo's place to know. They weren't friends.

"I like women." Mimi looked up. "I'm not sure to what extent. But I—" Their gazes met and Mimi blushed. "I do like women." She looked down again.

Leo put the last of the dishes away.

"Want to watch another movie?"

Without vocalizing her answer, Mimi nodded.

*

"I'm bored." It was later and they were sitting in the sofa after watching yet another movie. The only movies Sandra had were films from the Pink Panther boxset, and Mimi seemed to be getting increasingly tired of Peter Sellers.

Leo wondered what went on in Mimi's head. She hadn't tried to run away for a long time now. Leo wondered what she was planning. She didn't dare the futile hope that Mimi was just waiting for the time to pass. Watching movies together had been a strange experience. At first Leo had been hypervigilant, but now, after the third movie they had watched together, she found herself relaxing. Even enjoying it.

She watched in silence as Mimi jumped up and started walking towards the curtains. They were a light fabric and dotted with small white flowers. Mimi turned back towards Leo with a raised eyebrow and a smile playing on her lips, still holding the curtain.

"No, you can't be serious!" Leo didn't know whether to laugh or to cry.

"Please!" Mimi's teasing smile was genuine. "The fabric is old but lovely. I want to make a long skirt out of it. Except I'd need a zipper too. Do you think your boss lady has some old clothes here? I'll strip them for parts like a stolen car."

Leo was still hesitating and Mimi clearly noticed. She sat down next to Leo on the sofa.

"Come on, don't tell me you don't want to get back at the person who made you having to deal with me."

Leo couldn't help but return Mimi's mischievous smile. She laughed. *You're not that bad,* she wanted to say but didn't. What she couldn't fight however, was the overwhelming wish to make Mimi keep smiling.

"Fine. But only this one curtain, do you hear me?"

Mimi's smile got even wider, and before either of them could react, she leaned forward and in one fluid move threw her arms around Leo's neck and pressed a quick kiss to Leo's cheek. When she pulled back her cheeks were red and her eyes wide.

Leo cleared her throat and looked away, feeling her own face heat up. She had no idea what to say. The look in her face was one of horror. Not a reaction Leo wanted her to have.

"Will you take the curtain down?" Mimi stood up. "I think you'll reach it easier than me. I'll go and find something with a zipper." Before Leo had a chance to answer, Mimi left the room and went up the stairs.

Leo got up from the sofa and reached for the metal line that held the curtains. She laughed softly to herself as she got it down and started taking the curtain off it. It was only when she folded it and put it on the sofa in a neat pile that she realized that Mimi was alone upstairs and maybe getting up to God knows what.

Leo was about to go after her when Mimi came running down the stairs and back into the living room carrying a pair of trousers and a button up shirt. She placed them on the sofa and looked up at Leo. Her smile faltered, and she visibly paled as they stared at each other.

"I could have run away." She sounded breathless, in shock. "I... I could have run away."

They stared at each other awkwardly. Leo didn't know what to say. She couldn't think of anything that was appropriate in their situation.

"Come on, let's make your skirt." Leo cleared her throat. "I'll help you carry."

She gathered up the curtain and carried it into the kitchen. She listened to Mimi's steps behind her, making sure that she was still following Leo into the kitchen.

When Mimi had sat down to start on the skirt, Leo's phone buzzed. She answered, not bothering to leave the room.

"Yes?" She listened to the dark female voice on the other end, gave an affirmative answer, and turned off the call.

"Further instructions?" Mimi was still leaning over the curtain, cutting and stitching and whatever else it was that she needed to do when making a skirt.

"No." Leo said. "Just that favor for a favor. A package that needs to be picked up in Cologne and delivered in Berlin so it'll be easy to combine it with... eh..."

"With me." Mimi sighed.

"Yeah." Leo's phone rang again.

This time it was Sandra, and they spoke in French. When she turned off the call, Mimi turned away from the curtain-skirt and looked up at Leo.

"Was that about me?"

"The money has been moved earlier than they thought and they want you on Wednesday instead of Thursday." Leo put her phone back in her pocket.

"Did you get in trouble for not answering the phone?" As if on cue, they both looked at the mobile that was still lying in the middle of the table.

"No." Leo took the phone and threw it on the floor. "I should probably destroy it now." She stepped on it with the heel of her foot.

"When are we leaving?"

"Tomorrow." To her surprise, Leo felt no joy or relief. "We will stay in Cologne one night and then continue to Berlin."

Mimi nodded thoughtfully.

"Whatever," she said. "I'll wear the skirt tomorrow." She turned to her sewing machine.

Chapter Fourteen

They were both solemn the next morning as they sat around the breakfast table. Leo's bag and Mimi's boxes were packed, and Mimi was wearing her new skirt with one of Leo's T-shirts on top. They ate in silence, Leo did the dishes and then they were out to the car.

"It feels like my vacation is over." Mimi's facial expression was equal parts surprised and apathetic. "It's so stupid. I should be happy, but…" she stopped talking and inhaled deeply.

"Maybe just a little bit stupid." Leo felt the same way. *We both need to get a grip.* This confusion wasn't good for either of them. She couldn't think of anything to say.

They got into the car. Leo looked up at the house, it looked abandoned. She wondered how long it would be until it was full of people again.

"I must have Stockholm syndrome or something." Mimi rolled her eyes. "I'm planning to sleep. Wake me when we get there. Or when it's time to eat." She closed her eyes and turned her face away from Leo.

*

Mimi slept for several hours, and when she woke up the traffic signs were in German, and they were inside a big city. Probably already in Cologne.

She had been in Germany several times growing up since her dad's businesses were based there, but she'd never stayed long enough to learn the language or to love the culture. She had never been in Cologne before. And, by the look it, it wasn't a town she would ever want to return to.

The streets looked like they had been arranged by a kindergarten class, old beautiful buildings carved from stone and wood, all muddled up with modern creations of glass and steel. Mimi pressed her face against the window; not to call for help this time, but to take it all in. The scenery was so absurd she couldn't decide if she found it beautiful or ugly.

"The city was bombed a lot during the Second World War," Leo said. "There weren't that many houses left. Since then they've been rebuilding quite slowly."

"It looks stupid." Mimi didn't want to say that she was intrigued by it. "How do you know?"

"I went to elementary school here."

Mimi turned her face to look at Leo. She couldn't believe that Leo had volunteered information about herself.

"What?" Leo laughed, surprising her again. "I was a child once too, you know. I didn't spawn like a video game enemy."

Mimi didn't know how to respond to that, so she said nothing. Instead she looked at the scenery outside. It was easier to think of Leo as something... less human. An enemy. A bad guy. Thinking of her as a child—Mimi shook her head. She wondered if Leo's parents were alive and if they knew what Leo did for living.

"I wonder if my parents are worried," she said out loud.

"Of course they are," Leo said right away. "Their daughter has been kidnapped."

"I suppose." But Mimi wasn't convinced. "They're probably going to blame me. That I did something that caused this."

"I don't know about that." Leo squirmed in her seat as if uncomfortable.

"And I'm not sure if they're worried," Mimi continued, "or if they even care. I'm the screw-up."

"They care. They paid the ransom," Leo seemed to think for a moment. "Why are you a screw-up? I thought you were your family's little princess."

"I was exaggerating." Mimi scratched the back of her neck. "I have a sister and a brother. My brother is a lawyer, works as my dad's company attorney for all those lawsuits he loves. He is also married to a cute little woman and they have three demon-spawn. My sister…." She closed her eyes. She didn't want to talk about Mandy, not now, not ever. "My sister is dead. Has been for many years. But when she was alive she was a dream daughter, always did as she was told, never talked back. She went on to study economics at university while I just wanted to sew. Oh, and she was also engaged. To a respectable man." Mimi made an impatient noise and fought against the instinct to run her fingernails over her now itching skull.

"You don't have to talk about them," Leo said. "Come on, calm down."

At first Mimi didn't understand why Leo had told her to calm down, but then she noticed how fast she was breathing and how she was scratching the back of her neck almost violently. She willed her hand to stop and let it fall to her lap.

"I want to stay in a hotel tonight." Mimi tried to calm her racing heart. "I'll behave."

Leo nodded.

"What kind of family do you come from?" Mimi asked. "I've told you about mine, it's only fair."

"My parents aren't poor criminals, if that's what you think." Leo looked thoughtful.

"I never said I thought so. Although that would have been my first guess. I could see that boss of yours promising you with wealth or travels, and you'd say yes just to escape your poverty."

Mimi's matter-of-fact tone seemed to annoy Leo.

"My boss tempted me with travels and freedom." Leo took a bottle of water from between them. "Not money." She took a sip from it.

"But the money is good?"

Leo laughed.

"I make more than you do. Why? Thinking of changing your line of work?"

"I like to have options," Mimi joked. "And I have to admit that if your boss lady came and tempted me with money and travels I'd say yes. And I'd be good at it too! I could pretend to be a fashionista travelling from place to place and—"

"And you'd yell or bat your eyelashes at anyone who questioned?"

"Now you're getting it!"

Laughter bubbled up through Mimi's chest. She didn't know why she was laughing. From the relief of not being as scared anymore. To keep herself from crying. *We're not friends, stop laughing.* But Mimi couldn't stop laughing.

"Seriously though," Mimi continued after wiping a stray tear from her eye. "You are way too obvious. The black jacket, your tattoo." She pointed at Leo's right hand where the words 'trust no one' were displayed. "Your whole demeanor. All you need is a pair of sunglasses and a big sign that says 'up to no good.'"

Leo raised her eyebrow.

"You honestly think you'd be better at it than me?"

"Of course." Mimi grinned. "I don't have your raw strength, of course, but I have other talents. Like flirting my way out of situations." She ended her sentence by winking.

"What makes you think I can't do that?" Leo looked like she was about to start laughing again. "With the right person, baby, oh, I can flirt." She was teasing, but her voice had dropped lower, and, despite herself, Mimi couldn't help reacting to that smooth voice. She shivered.

"See," she said in an attempt to keep her cool. "You're terrible at your job. I'm sure the first rule is don't call your prisoner 'baby.'"

"Yeah." Leo was still smiling but the joking gleam in her eyes disappeared. "You're probably right about that."

Mimi chuckled one last time and then quieted down too. The boundaries that had once been so clear between them were getting blurry. She should have hated it, and yet she didn't. She started feeling sick and wanted to focus on something else.

"What's that?"

She pointed at a dark and pointy building that rose over the rest of the town. It looked black, dirty. A little bit scary.

"That's the Cologne Cathedral."

"Can we go and look at it?"

"What?" A car cut in front of them, and Leo slammed on the breaks. "Fuck. Idiots."

"I want to visit the Cologne Cathedral." *When in doubt, make demands.* "I doubt I will ever want to visit Cologne again after this, so I want to see it." Mimi knew she was pushing it; she didn't think that Leo would actually agree. She couldn't believe her eyes when Leo turned to the left and changed their course.

"Really?" She could feel herself smiling widely. She didn't even want to see the stupid, scary-looking cathedral. She just wanted to prove that she had some semblance of power.

"Yes, really. But we're walking to the top. All the 533 steps to the top of the tower."

"533 steps?" Mimi's smile faltered. "Are you serious?"

"Yes."

*

The cathedral was beautiful inside. There was no denying it. Mimi knew she had just asked in order to get Leo to do something for her, but once she had entered it, she was happy that this was what she had asked for.

There was so much *space* inside. It made Mimi feel like the ceiling actually reached all the way to heaven. Tinted windows let in soft light, bathing the whole cathedral in a yellow glow that seemed to envelop both Leo and Mimi like a warm blanket.

"Have you been in here before?" They were alone, and yet Mimi spoke in a hushed tone. She didn't want to disturb the sense of peace.

"Yes. With school once or twice. It's a German landmark." Leo grabbed Mimi's hand. "Come on, let's walk to the top."

Mimi didn't let Leo hold her hand, she wanted to walk independently, but she followed Leo. She couldn't believe that Leo actually wanted them to walk up to the top, but there was no way she was backing down. She would rather die than admit defeat.

The stairway was claustrophobic, and at first Mimi didn't like it. It was like climbing a stone tube. Thin windows let in minimal light here and there, but it wasn't enough.

"You okay?" Mimi didn't know how many steps they had climbed when Leo turned around and looked at her. "We're about half-way now, I think."

"I'm okay." Mimi sucked in air between her teeth. She was getting a bit out of breath, but she would never admit that. "Just keep walking." She wanted to get to the top now.

By the time she had gotten used to the continuous carousel of stairway, looking at Leo's back for comfort and motivation, they reached a steel cage with binoculars, looking out over Cologne below. And as ugly as Cologne had seemed down there, up here it was breathtaking.

Mimi walked right up to the net, put her fingers through it, and pulled her face close. She opened her eyes wide, wanting to take it all in. The odd little houses down there. The large river. The bridge. And in the distance, far, far away, the edge of the town, disappearing in a sunlit haze. She turned around, wanting to share this with Leo, share it with someone.

Leo was standing close to the stairs, as far away from the net that she could get.

"What's wrong with you?" Mimi waved for her to come closer. "Come and look, it's beautiful."

"No, thank you." Leo's smile was mild when she shook her head. "I don't like heights."

Mimi's mouth dropped.

"Then why on earth did you suggest we go up here?"

Leo's mouth twitched, and she looked so melancholic Mimi wished Leo was small enough for Mimi to pick her up and put her in her pocket for safekeeping.

"I wanted you to see it."

Mimi swallowed back sudden tears. She turned toward the view again. She wanted to carry the sight with her.

"Let's go." She walked ahead of Leo on the way down. She didn't want to look at her face anymore.

*

After Leo had picked up a small package waiting for them in an alleyway, they ate a fancy dinner in their car that consisted of grilled chicken, cheese, and bread before looking for somewhere to sleep in the center of Cologne.

Once they had found an appropriate hotel, they had to spend quite some time finding a parking space. Mimi had never seen such traffic or parking culture. On some streets there were even two rows of parking. It was funny to see Leo becoming increasingly frustrated. When she exclaimed, "I should have remembered that the best way to get a parking space in Cologne is buying a car that's already parked in one," Mimi burst out laughing, forgetting, for the moment, that she had decided not to laugh or smile at stuff Leo said anymore.

They soon found themselves checking into a hotel. It was late now, and Mimi didn't have a single thought of escaping. As nice as Leo had been, Mimi had no doubt that if she tried to run away Leo would find her way back to the stern kidnapper she had been in the beginning.

Things felt wrong and strangely domestic as they took turns taking showers, brushing their teeth, and getting ready for bed. Leo handed her a T-shirt and a fresh pair of underwear for Mimi to sleep in. They crawled under the covers and turned the light off with no words said between them. There were no talks of ropes or handcuffs. Mimi was apparently allowed to sleep without restraints this night. Maybe Leo felt as tired as she did herself.

Mimi was indeed tired, a little bit cold, and whenever she looked at Leo she felt strange. *I can't wait for this strange week to be over.* She closed her eyes, hoping that sleep would come quickly, but relaxing was harder than she had thought. She waited patiently, but her heart didn't slow down, and her skin thrummed with energy. She didn't know what it was that she wanted to do. Run maybe.

"I can't sleep," she whispered into the dark after what felt like an eternity.

Leo yawned. Then the mattress dipped behind her and Mimi was enveloped in strong arms, pulled against a warm body with her ears against Leo's heartbeat.

"Sleep," Leo murmured. "Tomorrow we'll go to Berlin and everything will be over."

Mimi was about to pull away when she felt her body relax. She closed her eyes and let herself mold against Leo's body. She could definitely sleep like this, she just didn't want to think about why that was. Eventually sleep came, and she fell into a dream that smelled like freshly-made baguettes, cigarettes, and mint gum.

Chapter Fifteen

What the hell is wrong with me? Mimi thought to herself as they dug into the hotel's intercontinental breakfast. Leo had smoked a cigarette before they had gone down, and she was looking particularly content. The food was delicious, Leo was fun and easy to talk with, and listening to the different languages around them was interesting. Nothing felt wrong. Everything felt right and that was precisely the problem.

I must really have Stockholm syndrome or something. She refused to remember waking up in Leo's arms, the bare skin of their arms almost having fused together. Instead she needed to remember that she wasn't on vacation with a friend, she was kidnapped, for crying out loud. This wasn't a business or pleasure affair, this was a crime. And she was the victim.

"I used to hate eggs," Leo said, causing Mimi to wake up from her thoughts. "I wonder why, they are so nice."

Mimi stared at her, it was hard to reconcile the friendly Leo with the evil person who had kidnapped her. Leo was a bit like a gentle giant, reserved but friendly. She was strong, of course, a criminal, and her sense of morality was questionable. But she had a funny side that Mimi liked, a sense of self and freedom that spoke to her. She also had an aura of mystery, a sense of secrecy that was more than intriguing. Mimi *liked her*. She would miss her. *Liked?*

Miss? What the hell? Mimi released the bread roll she had been holding. It fell to her plate with a thud that made Leo look up.

"What's wrong?"

Mimi had to get out of there. *Now.* She needed to run away right now, run all the way back to London. Once home she would call her dad and tell him that she was free so that maybe he didn't have to waste money on her. He would appreciate that.

"I have to go to the bathroom." She stood up and didn't look at Leo before turning around and walking away. Before leaving the breakfast hall, she grabbed another piece of bread, not caring what Leo thought. If she managed to run away now she wanted to be able to eat something later.

"Mimi!" Leo called out behind her, but Mimi didn't care. Instead she sped up and broke into a run, turning not toward the bathrooms but the hotel exit.

"Mimi, stop!" Leo had caught up with her and was right behind her now.

Mimi turned around and threw the bread roll right in Leo's face. Then she ran. She had almost reached the door when Leo caught up and grabbed a hold of her arm. Mimi burst out in tears.

"I'm sorry." Tears flowed down her cheeks. "I'm sorry. I'm sorry." She didn't know why she was apologizing or crying. She just couldn't stop.

"It's okay." Leo didn't sound angry or annoyed, she just opened her arms, and Mimi gratefully fell into them. She continued to cry, her face pressed into the crook of Leo's neck.

"Your dad's money has already been transferred," Leo whispered into her hair. "There is no point in running now. We can leave right now and not stop until we've reached Berlin. After that you never have to see me again."

"What about your other package?"

Leo shook her head.

"You're more important."

Leo probably meant that Mimi was worth more money or something like that, but it didn't matter. Mimi's heart was beyond listening to reason. She didn't care what anyone in the hotel foyer thought, she clung to Leo and cried her eyes out.

"You've got what you want," she mumbled into Leo's jacket. "Give me your phone. I'll call my dad, say that I'm fine. You can let me go now. You don't have to take me there."

"I'm sorry." Leo hugged her, properly, with both arms around her body and her chin on top of Mimi's head. It was the best, and the worst, hug Mimi had ever received.

*

"I appreciate you wanting to get me to Berlin as fast as possible," Mimi said. "But that doesn't mean we're not going to stop for lunch, right?"

Leo chuckled and gave her a fond look before turning her gaze to the road. They had been driving for a little bit less than an hour.

"We can eat anything you want."

"Don't say that," Mimi replied. "What if I say something like gluten-free pizza or unicorn steak?"

"Are you?"

"Gluten-free pizza is crap unless you make it yourself, and unicorns are too beautiful to eat, not counting imaginary, so I suppose you're safe."

Mimi was mildly bored. They had about two hours left to Berlin, and, despite the promise of a nice lunch, she felt restless. She didn't feel like sleeping like she had on the other road trips.

"Do you want to play a car game?"

Leo shook her head.

"Nope. *Non. Nein. Hayir*. I don't do car games. Most of them are pathetic, all of them boring."

Mimi sighed. She tried just looking out of the window, staring at the houses and people flying by, they hadn't even left Cologne yet. Her gaze drifted from the window and onto the glove compartment. She reached forward and opened it, but it was empty, not even car-papers. She sighed again.

"You can look through my bag if you'd like," Leo said.

Mimi raised one of her eyebrows. "Don't you have a gun in there?"

Leo reached to the seat behind her with just one hand on the wheel and pulled her bag onto her lap. She reached into it and took her gun out. She looked at it quickly, perhaps to check that the safety was on, and then she placed it between her legs on the seat. She then handed the bag to Mimi.

"Knock yourself out."

Mimi opened the bag and looked inside. Clothes, an iPad, a small toiletry bags, a couple of books, and things that weren't visible from the top.

"Is this everything you own?"

"Pretty much," Leo said. "I don't really have a home of my own, so owning a lot of things make no sense. I do have a small storage space, though, where I have a few more things."

"I like to travel, but I think I would go crazy if I didn't have a home to go to sometimes." Mimi continued looking through the things. She thought of taking out the iPad, but her hand touched a small bundle of photographs that she grabbed instead. She was about to look through all of them when a figure in the first photo made her mouth open in surprise.

"Leo! Who is this person?"

She held out the photo so Leo could see it. It pictured Leo and a couple of other people, including a woman that was very familiar to Mimi.

Leo glanced at it quickly.

"Who do you mean? It's just a couple of my coworkers, none of importance."

Mimi shook her head impatiently.

"This." She pointed at the curvy, black haired woman on the photograph. "This woman is a close friend of my dad's. Her name is Sandra Sousa." She thought for a little while. "Is she the one who ordered my kidnapping? She has her fucking arm around you in the photograph. Girlfriend of yours?"

Instead of answering, Leo drove to the side of the road and stopped the car violently. She took the photograph from Mimi's hand and looked at it for a long time without saying anything.

"Just tell me the truth." Mimi had had enough. "I know her. When I get home I can ask Dad to call her himself and ask of her involvement."

"That's Sandra," Leo said without looking up. "My boss." She kept staring at the photograph.

"Boss lady who lured you away with freedom and travels?" Mimi grabbed the photo and looked at it again. "I pictured her blonde and skinny for some reason. Not…." Mimi's Aunt Sandra.

"Does Sandra know you?" Leo's voice was soft.

"She practically watched me grow up." Mimi couldn't take her eyes off of the photograph. "When I was little I even called her Auntie Sandra. She's been friends with my dad for forever. She *knows* me." She pursed her lips. "If she's your boss, she's probably the one who kidnapped me. Poor dad."

*

Leo's head spun. What the hell had she just stumbled upon? What conspiracy was she uncovering? Sandra had money, a steady income, and several houses. She didn't have any reason to kidnap her friend's daughter for ransom. It didn't make any sense. Nothing about this situation made any sense. There had to be something bigger behind all of this. Something other than money.

"So what are we going to do now?" Mimi was looking at her with raised eyebrows and a pointed look in her face.

"What do you mean?" Leo still couldn't process what was happening.

"Well, clearly there are things your boss lady didn't tell you. Don't you want to get to the bottom of this?"

"Not really." Leo put the photograph back in her bag and threw it to the seat behind her.

Mimi smiled again, the sweet, devious smile that Leo had gotten addicted to during the past couple of days. She knew that she was about to be talked into something, and she didn't have the will to guard herself against it. She didn't stand a chance. Not when the foundations of her entire world were shaking.

"Leo," Mimi said, "you only have two choices. Either you continue, you deliver me to my dad, and we hope for the best. I'll name you, Sandra, and describe that man we stayed with before. Your life is ruined. Or we think of another solution. Let me get back to London. I can call my dad when I'm on the way there and tell him that I'm fine. I'll leave your name out of it." Mimi smiled again but this time it looked more genuine.

Mimi liked her. Why she did, Leo didn't know, but it didn't make it any less true. She knew instinctively that Mimi liked her. What Mimi wanted most was her freedom, and if Leo delivered her to her dad, Mimi would have lost part of that freedom. Leo was sure of it. And she didn't want that. Leo didn't want that because Leo liked Mimi back.

"I'd go with the second." Leo scratched the back of her head. Going against Sandra was more than a little bit scary. "I want to let you go home, Mimi, honestly I do. I just don't know if it's possible. It's my job to—" Mimi put a hand over Leo's mouth.

"You kidnapped me." Her gaze was deadly. "You made me fall and hit my head. You have drugged me multiple times. You've locked me inside a trunk. That wasn't okay. Do you want to continue? Should I scream until you drug me again? Will you beat me up if I struggle too much? Maybe shoot me in the knee so I can't run?"

"Of course not." Leo spoke into her palm. The thought of harming Mimi, of hitting her, was too much to bear. Leo didn't want to drug her or lock her in the trunk again. They were at an impasse. Leo only had one choice, and, for once, it was the right choice. The moral choice.

"Do you want me to take you to Berlin?"

"No." Mimi shook her head and removed her hand. "I want to go home. To London."

Leo nodded.

"I'll drive you to Berlin, you can take the train from there. We're almost there anyway."

"Thank you." Mimi sank back into her seat. Breathing deeply. "What are you going to do?"

"I don't know." Leo stepped on the gas. "Disappear somewhere. I'll figure it out, I always do."

*

Way too quickly for Mimi's liking they found themselves by a train station in Berlin. Leo had bought her a ticket, a sandwich, and a bottle of water.

"I'll package your sewing machine and send it to you," Leo said as they awkwardly stared at each other.

"Thank you." It was an incredibly sweet gesture, but Mimi didn't care about the sewing machine right at that moment. "I'll... ummh." There was nothing Mimi could say. *I'll miss you? I'll write you?* What do you say to your kidnapper?

She reached out with her hand and traced the letters of Leo's tattoo. *Trust no one.* Leo's hand was so cold. She fought against the urge to press a kiss to the small hollow between Leo's thumb and forefinger. Their eyes met again.

"Your tattoo is lame." She flashed Leo a brilliant smile, turned around, and started walking towards the train trying to ignore the stabs of sadness she felt.

She was finally free. She could go back to her old life. Paige was going to be so relieved to hear from her again. And her store! Mimi would need to do so many... Leo. Mimi stopped walking. Turned around. Across the platform Leo was still standing there, an unreadable expression in her face. The expression turned into confusion as Mimi returned to her.

"You have something more to say about my tattoo I take it?" Leo's smile was hopeful. It was cute, Mimi realized. Very cute, just like Leo herself.

"Oh, I have plenty to say, but that'll have to wait." Mimi didn't want to waste any more time. "Aren't you going to get into trouble?"

Leo sighed and that was all the answers Mimi needed.

"That's not really any of your business." Leo moved her gaze so that Mimi could no longer meet it with her own.

"Of course it's my business if it's because of me." Mimi wanted to take Leo by the shoulders and shake her.

"I kidnapped you." Leo was whispering now. "I'm a criminal, remember? I'm quite sure you aren't supposed to care about what happens to me once I let you go."

"And I'm quite sure that if you had said no to this job I would have been treated much, much worse and not been set free." She took Leo's hand and held it until Leo met her gaze. "You're a terrible kidnapper, Leo, but that allows me to be a terrible kidnappee and care about what will happen to you."

"So what do you suggest we do?" Leo gave her hand a light squeeze and Mimi smiled at the sensation.

"I suggest we see this through as planned. Just bring me to my dad's house." *I'll figure it out when we get there.*

Chapter Sixteen

They parked a couple of blocks away from Mimi's dad's house, neither of them wanting to continue all the way there. Leo didn't like the idea of walking into the arms of Mimi's dad, and she didn't like the idea of giving Sandra's name to anyone. It didn't feel right.

She glanced at Mimi, who was sitting on the passenger seat, her expression unreadable. Leo couldn't trust her, not one bit. It had been different when they had been talking, it had been different at the station when they had been so close to hugging, so close to some form of mutual understanding. Now when it was time for Mimi to go and see her dad, Leo didn't want her to. Who knew what she would tell.

"I have to make a phone call," she mumbled. "Will you wait here?"

Mimi looked like she wanted to argue, so Leo hurried to open her mouth again.

"You can go and talk to your dad." She scratched the back of her hair. "But I need to warn Sandra. I just have to." Breaking free wasn't easy, and she still felt like she needed something.

"Why can't you call her here? I promise to be quiet."

"No, sorry."

Before Mimi had had a chance to say anything else, Leo got out the car, taking the keys with her. She didn't bother locking the doors or anything, but she didn't want to leave the keys inside. Then she took out her phone and clicked her way to Sandra's number.

"Leo?" Sandra got straight to the point. "Why are you calling me? Has something happened? Are you in Berlin yet?"

"Yes," Leo said, "we're in Berlin, but I have to tell you something." Leo took a deep breath. She wasn't sure what angle she wanted to play. She had never before gone against Sandra's wishes. "The game is up. Mimi found a photo of you, recognized who you are. She's going to name you to her dad."

Leo twitched when Sandra swore loudly.

"Damn. How could you fuck this up? Can't you do anything right?" Panic gripped Leo by the throat and disappointment in herself made it hard to breathe. "The father isn't the problem." *What?* "It was his fucking idea for crying out loud. But now the girl can identify me? What if she runs to the police?"

"Her… dad's idea?" Leo didn't know what to say to that.

"Yes, of course!" Sandra snorted. "He's tried to get her home for years. But now, you idiot, you let her see my face."

Leo remained quiet. *I must be dreaming.* The instinct to say anything to make Sandra less angry with her couldn't win this time.

"Damn it, Leo." Sandra continued. "Is she still in your possession?"

Possession? Leo glanced at Mimi in the car. *No,* was the proper answer. She didn't possess Mimi anymore. Mimi was her own person. Finally.

"Yes."

"Good. Keep her for a while longer, do whatever you have to. I need to call her father and figure this out. Fuck, Leo. Don't screw up one more time, you hear me?"

"But… why?" Leo didn't think she would ever feel normal again. There had been too many surprises for one day. "What does he want with her?"

"That's none of our business. Just do your job, don't worry about the rest. Why don't you take a bit of a vacation after this? You have earned it, after all. I know that Mimi can be a bit of a pest."

She's not been a pest, Leo thought but didn't say.

"Okay," she said, unsure what else there was that she could say. "Speak to you later."

"I'll pay you next time we meet." Sandra turned off the call.

Leo had more than one decision to make, and it was making her skin crawl. Her life was usually so easy. She opened the car door and slid into the seat next to Mimi.

"What did she say?"

"What kind of person is your dad?" Leo asked instead of answering.

Mimi's smile faltered and she frowned.

"He can be controlling at times," she said in a small voice. "And when I was little, he loved to think of colorful punishments when we did something he didn't want. But he's gotten better, last time we talked on the phone he even asked how my business was going. He is still very adamant that I go to Berlin and live with them, but," she sighed. "I hope that one day he will change."

Leo shook her head. She couldn't believe that she had helped in the process of imprisoning Mimi in such a way, of taking away her freedom for longer than just a week. Whoever Mimi was, it was clear that she loved her freedom, that she valued it over anything else. She valued it over a good place to live and having enough money. Leo didn't want to take it from her. And just like that, she had decided.

She started the car and drove off.

"This is them," Mimi said as they got closer to her dad's house. "I can't believe he hasn't sold the house, it used to be a nice neighborhood but—" They drove past it. "What are you doing? I thought we were stopping?"

Leo glanced at her quickly, she realized she had done this precise thing to Mimi before, driving off without her knowing where they were going. But this time it was different.

"I'll tell you what's going on, but let's get out of Berlin first."

"No," Mimi shook her head. "You have to tell me first."

"I don't want to upset you, not until we're safely out of Berlin." Leo didn't think that anyone would be coming after them, but she wanted to make sure. Now that she had made up her mind, it was important to get away from Berlin as fast as possible.

"I'm not made of porcelain. You can tell me." Mimi lowered her voice. "Please tell me."

"Your dad is behind it." Leo didn't think she had to specify what.

"What do you mean?" Mimi's tone turned shrill. "No, he isn't."

"Yes, he is." Leo unconsciously stepped on the gas a bit. "According to Sandra, he wants you back home."

Mimi turned silent.

*

She wanted to be furious. Mimi wanted anger to drown the feelings of anguish and sadness that were rising on the inside. Anger had been her armor for so long, and without it she felt like she was going to drown. She tried to recall the last time she had spoken to her dad. *He had been fine with it,* she thought, *he was finally fine with it!* Clearly it had been a lie. Everything had been a lie. She wanted to hate him for it, but couldn't, so then all she wanted to do was lie down and cry.

She barely paid attention as Leo drove them through Berlin and then stopped the car outside *Berlin Hauptbahnhof,* the station. She sat completely still until Leo stopped the car and got out. Mimi got out as well, her brain on autopilot.

"I'm going to get us two tickets, okay?" She took Mimi's hand and held it gently as they made their way through the crowd toward the ticket booth.

"Where are we going?" Mimi felt numb. "Back to London?"

"Not tonight, sweetheart." Leo squeezed her hand. "We're going to Gransee. Just for tonight. To hide."

"What's Gransee?"

"I used to go there with my dad when I was a child." They had arrived at the ticket booth and Leo took a step forward.

"Hallo. Zwei Tickets nach Gransee, bitte." She tried to pull her hand from Mimi's hold, but Mimi held on.

"Gransee, das wäre der Regional-express. Der nächste kommt um 14.44 Uhr, Gleis 6. Das sollten Sie noch schaffen."

She didn't listen as Leo and the man in the booth kept talking. Eventually Leo turned and looked at her until Mimi let her hand go. Leo paid and grabbed the tickets.

"The next train is in ten minutes, come on."

She took a hold of Mimi's hand again and led her through the train station. Before Mimi could even register what was happening, she was sitting on a train next to Leo.

"We forgot my sewing machine." She looked with jealousy at Leo's bag, which was by her side like usual.

"The car is locked." Leo's voice was sympathetic. "They'll still be there later. We just had to leave quickly."

"Where are we going?"

"To a little town called Gransee." Leo got the tickets out and looked at them. "It's a small town. Historical. My dad used to take me there a lot." It sounded like there was more to the story but Mimi couldn't focus on that right now.

"Are there people after us?" She closed her eyes. Her life had always been a little bit dramatic, but this really took the price.

"There could be," Leo said. "I didn't want to take a risk. We'll go to Gransee, find somewhere to stay the night and just lay low."

"What does that even mean?" Mimi groaned and leaned forward. She cradled her head in her hands. "You said you would take me home."

"I want to get you home. I just haven't figured everything out yet."

"That's an understatement." Mimi felt the anger finally come to the surface, unfortunately for Leo, she was the only target there. "You're utterly useless in figuring things out, you know that, right? You can't think for yourself. Always following orders."

Leo looked up at her, and the hurt Mimi could see in her eyes made it all worth it. She wanted to hurt Leo, she wanted to pierce and cut until Leo hurt as much as she did.

Mimi deserved to be in a bad mood, she deserved to be bitchy. Her own dad had tried to kidnap her, for crying out loud. And Leo had executed the order.

"Unless somebody tells you something, you don't think about it. Some kidnapper you are."

"Shut your mouth," Leo hissed. "Do you want to everyone to hear?"

"Oh, so now you care?" Mimi felt like laughing. "You're the worst kidnapper ever. You showed me your face from the beginning. I know your name. You've given me so many opportunities to escape that it's pathetic…." She felt tears burning at the corners of her eyes and she panicked. She didn't want to cry. She *wasn't* going to cry. "I hate you, this is all your fault." She managed, then she broke down sobbing. She lifted her fist and beat it weakly against Leo's chest, she raised it to repeat the movement but was carefully enveloped in a strong embrace.

"Shh." Leo's voice was infuriatingly soothing. "It's okay."

It was a lie. But Mimi appreciated it. She struggled, pushing out with her arms, she didn't want the comfort that was so freely offered. Instead of letting her go, Leo tightened her arms and Mimi found her nose pressed into Leo's clavicle. Her arms got tired, and without really wanting too, Mimi's arms fell around Leo's waist and she held on. Leo held her like that for a few minutes, and when Mimi stopped sobbing she let go.

"Well, this is awkward." Mimi cleared her throat. "I'm sorry for crying all over you." She looked at the wet spot on top of Leo's shirt.

"That's okay."

Mimi turned and looked out of the window. She stayed quiet as the conductor came to check on their tickets, then she turned back towards Leo.

"How much were the tickets?"

"13.60 euros." Leo took out her bag and put the tickets in there.

"I'll pay you back later," Mimi said. "You've paid a lot for me during these couple of days."

Leo raised an eyebrow in her direction.

"Paying for myself is important." Mimi looked down. "Our circumstances don't matter." Leo didn't answer so Mimi kept talking. "I don't care what people think, but I have pride. I will ask for favors when I need them, but I never ask for money. I'll starve before I ask for money. So when we're out of this, I want to pay you back. I need to. For myself."

Chapter Seventeen

When they arrived at Gransee train station, they first walked without a goal. Gransee wasn't what Leo remembered from when she was a child. Her trips to Gransee had been magical, but now, through the eyes of an adult, it was normal. There were still old buildings, and it was still a beautiful historical place, but otherwise it seemed so ordinary.

Eventually they found a small bed-and-breakfast where they entered and got a room. They went up the stairs in silence, finding their room. Neither of them had said a word to the other since leaving the train. They both had things to process. Leo still couldn't believe that she had gone against Sandra's orders like that. It felt surreal.

"I want to take a shower." Mimi took her shoes off and pulled her fingers through her hair.

Leo nodded without replying. If Mimi wanted to be alone, Leo would respect that. She needed to be alone too. To think.

While Mimi headed into the shower, Leo sat down on the bed and turned on the TV. She flipped through the channels with the sound turned down low and listened to the drumming water from the shower. She kept listening as the water stopped and Mimi started humming. Leo couldn't for the life of her understand what was making Mimi hum, but she was thankful for the noise.

"I know what we should do." Mimi came out of the bathroom.

All she was wearing was a towel wrapped around her body, and Leo was momentarily distracted by Mimi's bare shoulders and the hair that fell down in black wet locks around Mimi's face.

"What?" She looked up when she realized that Mimi had continued talking. "I'm sorry. What do you think we should do?"

"Go to South America." Mimi pointed at Leo's bag, and when Leo gave her a curt nod, she went up to it. Took out a pair of underwear. "Or Australia. Or Canada. Let's just run." She re-entered the bathroom but kept talking with the door open. "Get away from your boss lady and my dad."

"And live on what?" Leo rubbed the back of her head. "Dress making? And you do know we need visas to move anywhere, right?"

"I didn't say my plan was perfect." Mimi came back into the room, this time with clothes on, drying her hair. Leo turned off the TV. "But at least I have a plan."

"Fine," Leo muttered. "We'll call that Plan B."

"Good." Mimi jumped and landed on the bed next to Leo. "What do you want to do now? We can have food later, right?"

Leo couldn't help but smile widely.

"I've never met a woman who loves food as much as you do. It feels like we're eating all the time. Where do you put it all?" She fought the impulse to reach out and tickle Mimi's lean stomach.

Mimi smiled, but a sad look came over her face.

"Mother used to tell me not to eat so much." She shook her head. "It's not womanly. And since I haven't always afforded to feed myself, it's made me very appreciative of food. Good food. Mmm, food." She smiled again and they laughed together.

"Seriously, though," Mimi said when the laughter subsided. "What are we going to do?"

Leo's smile faltered.

"I don't know."

"I meant for dinner." Mimi winked.

Leo burst out laughing.

"Okay, I'll go and get something for us to eat. Want to wait here?" Leo didn't think that anybody in Gransee was looking for Mimi, but she was rather safe than sorry.

"You trust that I won't run away?"

"I do trust you." Leo put her hands in the pocket of her leather jacket. "But if you want to run away it's your right."

"You're an idiot." But the words were full of affection, not scorn. "You are the worst kidnapper ever. Truly idiotic." Mimi's eyes turned gentle as she looked at Leo. "Come back soon, okay?"

*

When Leo came back thirty minutes later, she was carrying boxes of potato salad and smoked salmon and Mimi actually cheered.

"Finally a proper meal." Mimi took the boxes from Leo's hands and brought them to the bed. "Do you have cutlery?"

Leo nodded.

"Check the bottom of the bag."

Mimi smiled when she found it.

"Come on." She patted the bed next to her. "If you don't, I'll eat it all without you."

Leo hurried to take off her shoes and jacket and sat down next to Mimi. Her movements were slow, almost pensive, as if she wasn't sure what was happening or what was expected of her.

Mimi handed her one of the boxes and a plastic spoon. She smiled at her, wanting to reassure her, comfort her. Then she dug in.

"Mmm." The food was absolutely divine. "Potato salad is the best thing on the planet."

Leo smiled crookedly but said nothing.

"No, but seriously," Mimi continued as soon as she had swallowed. "Actually, anything that involves potato. Potato salad, potato gratin, mash, fries, vodka." She fell silent to inhale another spoonful.

Afterward she held out the box so Leo could put her spoon in it too. She also reached out to grab a thin piece of salmon with the tips of her fingers.

"Do you feel like a mutt sometimes?"

Leo raised one of her eyebrows.

"You said your mom is Turkish. And your dad is German. Do you feel like a mutt? Without your pedigree."

Leo's eyes went wide.

"No!" She swallowed visibly. "Do you?"

She chewed the salmon quickly so she could keep talking.

"My mother's family have always been very clear on the fact that we're not Japanese. And it's like I'm wearing a huge sign telling everyone that I'm not European or American. I am neither. Nothing. A mutt."

Leo sighed, but she looked relaxed. During the short time that Mimi had known her, Leo had always had a tightness around her eyes and held her mouth in a thin line.

She looked relaxed now, leaning back on her elbows with a lazy smile playing on her lips.

"I've never thought about it that way," she said eventually. "Most of the time I was just German. My mom died when I was a teenager, and all I have left of her is this—" She grabbed a handful of her dark hair. "And a language that has helped me as a criminal." She sighed again, and her smile turned wistful. "That's not true. I also inherited her restlessness, her unhappiness, and her loneliness." She looked away.

Mimi stared at her. She hadn't expected Leo to confess something so intimate and was now unsure of what to say.

"Do you feel German?" She kept her voice soft.

"I guess." Leo shook her head. "But I haven't lived here properly for over a decade. I've been too busy, travelling. Moving stuff."

"What about Christmas? Or…" Mimi eyed her curiously. "Eid?"

Leo smiled.

"My dad used to invite me for Christmas and Easter but I didn't go." Their eyes met. "He gave up a few years ago."

"Is he still alive?"

Leo nodded.

"I wish…" Leo shook her head. "Never mind."

"You should call him." Mimi didn't fight against the impulse to reach out and grab Leo's hand. It did feel a bit strange to hold hands, but Mimi didn't care. Her whole life had been one big uncomfortable situation. "I'm serious." She smiled. "If you had a good dad, if…" She licked her lips searching for the proper words. "If you miss him, you should call him."

"I wish it was that easy."

"You idiot." Mimi smiled again. She was quickly learning that smiling at Leo was one of her favorite activities. Every time she smiled at her it was as if somebody lit a light inside Leo's eyes. "Kidnapping people is hard; calling someone is definitely easy."

Leo grinned.

"Well, when you put it that way…."

Mimi got up and gathered the now empty boxes, plastic forks, and napkins. She put them back into the plastic bag, closed it with a knot, and threw it next to the door.

Leo turned around and lay down on her stomach, pointing the remote at the TV. Mimi leaned against the wall and looked at her. Her friend. Not her kidnapper. Her friend. What a strange week this was.

"What are we watching?" She walked up to Leo and joined her on the bed.

"Silly German movie. It's called '*3 Türken & ein Baby.*' Three Turks and a Baby. I've seen it before, it's fun."

Mimi smiled and lay with her stomach down on the bed. Their shoulders bumped. The sun was setting outside, and Mimi wondered where the day had gone. Had she really tried to run away from Leo that very morning? It felt like forever ago. She glanced at the woman next to her. They were strangers and yet their friendship had an intimate taste to it. Like they knew each other very well. *I guess kidnapping will do that to you.*

She didn't understand any of the movie, there were no subtitles, but she laughed when Leo laughed, reacted when Leo reacted and, when it finished with a clearly happy ending, Leo explained to her what had happened.

Mimi couldn't remember the last time she had enjoyed herself so much. The last time she had felt so relaxed. It had been years, if ever. Her life had always been just a little bit stressful, a little bit uncomfortable, a little bit strange.

Leo yawned and turned off the TV.

"Let's just sleep. Maybe we'll figure something out tomorrow."

*

Within minutes they were lying down in separate beds. In the dark.

Mimi should have felt elated. She was sleeping in a bed, on her own, without being handcuffed. She turned to the side and put one leg outside the cover. She didn't feel relieved. She felt restless and kind of lonely. She looked over at Leo's bed, at the steady rise and fall of her kidnapper's chest.

She's not my kidnapper anymore, though. Mimi shook her head with a quiet chuckle. Leo was her friend now. Her gorgeous, reserved, criminal friend that she had met during the most terrible circumstances. They couldn't—shouldn't—be friends, but they were anyway. She knew this.

She twisted on the bed and stared up in the ceiling. Friends. Such a strange term. More than just *human I tolerate.*

Leo whimpered softly in her sleep, making Mimi look at her again. Leo was definitely more than just tolerable. And she was in trouble. Because of Mimi.

It didn't feel right; she had been a pawn just as much as Mimi had been. It was time for them both to rebel, to take their freedom. Take what they wanted.

What did Mimi want? Her freedom. But not from Leo. Never from Leo.

Mimi put her hand on her abdomen. Pulled her borrowed T-shirt up and put her hand against the bare skin of her stomach. Her skin felt tight, and when her finger traced a circle around her navel, her skin prickled. Of course that's what her restlessness was.

She was aroused. Badly so. She had felt so many different emotions during the past days that it wasn't strange her body needed some form of physical outlet.

She glanced over to Leo. It was just about physical release, she told herself. She wanted Leo. And when Mimi wanted something, she took it. Leo owed her that much, no? Not that she would insist if Leo rejected her. But Mimi didn't think that Leo would.

Having decided, she lifted the covers, slipped out, and headed over to Leo's bed.

She couldn't believe her own boldness as she lifted Leo's covers and laid down next to her. She didn't want to scare her, so she gently pressed her lips against Leo's cheek and paid attention to any reactions. When Leo just sighed softly, Mimi continued by pressing her lips to Leo's. She just pecked them at first, but when Leo responded, she opened her lips gently. But before she managed to initiate a proper kiss, Leo spoke.

"What are you doing?" Leo's voice was sharp in the dark. It made Mimi wish the room wasn't so dark. She had no way of seeing Leo's facial expression, and it was making her a little bit nervous. *What am I doing?* Even Mimi realized that it was insanity. It was too late to back out now.

They sat up. Leo radiated heat, the familiar scent of cigarette and mint making Mimi want to kiss her again.

"I'm kissing you." She forced confidence into her voice. "Isn't that obvious?" She lifted her hand and traced the neckline of Leo's large T-shirt. She felt goosebumps under her finger and smiled triumphantly. "I want to spend the night with you. I want to be with you. Can we?" It didn't matter how much she wanted to, she couldn't sound anything other than shy at her question.

Leo gasped as Mimi placed her palm on her naked shoulder, inside the shirt. Mimi couldn't help it, her hand couldn't stop exploring.

"You... you do? But why?" Leo's harsh tone was gone. Instead the tone of her voice was unreadable, and the question caught Mimi off guard. "You shouldn't." She was out of breath.

"Do I need to have a reason?"

Leo produced a surprised laugh.

"How about this whole situation? How about I'm your kidnapper? How about we're on the run? How about...."

Mimi placed her palm over Leo's mouth, silencing her. The reversal of roles wasn't lost on her, and she was grateful that Leo couldn't see her triumphant smile.

"How about I find you gorgeous, a little bit dim-witted in a way I find attractive, and I have been dreaming about kissing you all day? Are those good enough reasons?"

She removed her hand from Leo's mouth.

"Uh, yeah. I think so." Leo's voice had taken on a husky quality that made Mimi's toes curl.

"Well, it's settled then." Mimi leaned forward and sealed their lips together properly. She didn't want to talk anymore. Now she wanted to get to know Leo.

"No, wait." Leo pulled back again. Mimi groaned in frustration.

Leo turned the light on. She put one finger underneath Mimi's chin and looked at her. Mimi was under scrutiny now and she wasn't sure she liked it.

"What?" she asked, a bit more aggressively than she had meant to.

"What are you trying to prove?" Leo seemed completely calm, there was only a slight blush on her cheeks that showed that she was affected at all.

"I'm… not…." Mimi bit her teeth together. How dare Leo? Mimi wasn't trying to prove anything.

"You've got your freedom." Leo's eyes shone. "You don't need to prove anything with me. You don't need to do this."

Mimi had had enough. She felt equal parts mortified and powerful when she pulled Leo's hand and pushed it against her, just hard enough so Leo could feel how wet she was.

"Does that feel like I have something to prove?" She hissed close to Leo's ear.

"No, it doesn't." Leo gasped and pulled away her hand as if she had been burned. "Are you sure?"

"I'm sure." Mimi tried to smile in a sultry manner but wasn't sure she pulled it off. "Do you want me?"

"Yes." Leo seemed to have lost whatever internal battle she had and now reached for Mimi.

They kissed and Mimi moved her fingers to Leo's back, inside the shirt, and scraped her nails between Leo's shoulder blades. Leo made a sound somewhere between a moan and a growl, which made Mimi's clit twitch. It felt like she was burning up and she couldn't get enough. She grabbed Leo's neck with her hand and pulled her closer. As soon as Leo was close enough, Mimi moved her mouth from Leo's and bit her neck. She wanted Leo to make the sound again. And again.

She was driving Leo crazy; that much was clear by the way Leo was writhing and grasping at her waist. At first that was enough. But pretty soon it wasn't.

"Wait." Mimi pulled back. She tugged at Leo's shirt. "Please, we need… naked… clothes." She wanted to slap herself for sounding so stupid.

Leo didn't seem to mind. She pushed Mimi away and pulled her own shirt off. Mimi sucked in breath through her teeth when taking in Leo's firm breasts above a defined abdomen. *It should be illegal to be that sexy,* she thought as she pulled her own T-shirt over her head. She also removed her underwear and motioned for Leo to do the same.

She rushed forward, ready to put her hands and mouth to the brown nipples that she couldn't stop looking at, but she was stopped by a hand on her shoulder.

"Mimi, wait!"

"No." Mimi shook her head and removed Leo's hand. "Can't wait."

They came together on the middle of the bed, arms around each other. Even Leo, who had tried to stop her, seemed to have no objections as she produced an enticing moan and pulled her closer. Mimi whimpered, it was feeling too good, and she pressed her lower body more firmly into Leo's. She gasped when Leo groaned and guided Mimi to straddle her thigh. Mimi pressed down on the firm muscle, no longer able to control her wanton movements. *This is insane,* she thought, *this is the woman who kidnapped you. Evil, evil, evil L—*

Leo's hands came to rest on her hips and a strangled sound escaped her.

"I… want…" Leo sounded like she was dying, her words coming out between strained pants. "… you… under me."

Mimi chuckled. She leaned forward and nipped at Leo's bottom lip.

"We don't always get what we want, do we now?"

But Mimi couldn't deny that the thought of having Leo's taut body on top of hers was something she would definitely have to revisit later. But first she wanted to drive Leo even crazier. Mimi felt drunk and she wanted more.

She leaned down and licked Leo's left nipple quickly, reveling in Leo's groan. She closed her lips around it and sucked gently. Leo's hands came to rest on top of her head, holding her against her breast. Leo rose her thigh, and Mimi ground harsher against it. She knew she could come like this, with Leo's nipple in her mouth and her center against Leo's firm thigh, but that was far from her goal. There were things she needed to do.

With one last kiss to Leo's hardened nipple, she kissed and licked her way down. She placed herself with her head between Leo's spread thighs.

"Mimi." Leo's hand came down on her shoulder. "You don't need to. I don't deserve—" She sounded sad.

"Shut up. I want to."

It didn't matter how they started. Maybe outside this room it mattered, but not right then and there. All that mattered in Mimi's mind was how Leo's scent was making her mouth water.

"I've never done this before." She had to say it. If she was going to rule Leo with pleasure, which was her goal, Leo needed to know. She sucked in breath through her nose and knew that if she could just get the hang of this, she would love it.

She looked up just in time to see Leo nod, acknowledging what Mimi had said, and drop her head on the pillow. Mimi smiled to herself and dived in.

She was uncharacteristically nervous but swallowed and tentatively let her tongue trace the outline of the slick flesh in front of her. Leo tensed and cried out above her. *Aha.* Following instincts, she closed her lips around the firm bud that was peeking out and practically begging for attention.

"Suck me." Leo groaned. "Yes… just like that. I'm not going to last long."

Mimi giggled as much as she could while never stopping the movements of her lips and tongue. There was also a growing feeling in her lower abdomen, and she pressed her hips into the mattress, desperate for some friction where she needed it the most.

"Mimi! I'm going to… fuck!"

Mimi was expecting feelings of triumph, that she would feel like winner, when Leo's orgasm burst against her lips. Instead another feeling rose in chest. She felt honored. When Leo cried out, and her hand came down to entwine with Mimi's, Mimi felt honored that she was allowed to see Leo this way. To feel her. To know her at her most vulnerable. She pressed her hips against the mattress, feeling like she was going to explode.

The movements of Leo's hips had slowed down, but she was trembling and her hands were hiding her face.

Mimi leaned back and wiped the lower part of her face with the back of her hand. She was ridiculously wet, more than she was allowed to be. She needed to gather her breath. It felt like something inside her was ready to snap. Some integral part of her was dissolving, the part that let her stay in control. She didn't want to know what would happen if she came undone. She couldn't afford to. Maybe she had had something to prove after all.

"Are you okay?"

Mimi looked up, Leo was looking at her with a questioning look in her face.

"Of course." But Mimi's voice wasn't as confident as she wanted it to be. She looked down, she didn't want to Leo to see her eyes. If she did, she would know. She would know that Mimi was breaking.

"Come up here." Leo pulled Mimi up by her arms and placed her face in Mimi's hair.

She made a content humming sound that annoyed Mimi to no end. It wasn't fair how that sound made Mimi feel inside.

"I want you inside me." Her voice broke. Mimi didn't want to cuddle. She couldn't cuddle. Not now.

Leo looked into her eyes as one of her hands travelled down Mimi's body and toward an obvious goal. Her eyes darkened with lust, and Mimi held her gaze, ignoring how her heart was beating with something resembling fear.

Leo kissed the top of her nose.

"I can stop anytime, okay? Just tell me and I will stop right away." She didn't say anything else, but instead started kissing Mimi's neck.

Mimi hummed in agreement even as she swallowed back tears. There would probably never be another time for them. There wouldn't be a next time. This was it. Her only chance to know Leo. Mimi's heart broke, and in the same time a resolve rose within her. If this was the only chance she got to be with Leo and have Leo be with her, she would appreciate it fully.

They kissed, their tongues moving together. Mimi whimpered when Leo finally came to lie on top of her. She had been right, the feeling of Leo's weight on top of her was lovely, and her legs parted willingly.

"Tell me if anything hurts, okay?"

Leo fingers parted her gently. She was ready, so very, very wet, but she was feeling nervous and tense and her muscles clenched around the welcome invasion. Mimi moaned, and her hands came up to rest on Leo's damp shoulders.

"Look at me." Leo's voice was pleading. "Be here with me."

Their eyes connected and Leo started stroking her. She kept her movements gentle, pushing into Mimi, their eyes never leaving one another. It was too much despite the gentle movements. Mimi felt her walls crumbling, and she tore her gaze away. With a hand to the back of Leo's head, she pulled her down until Leo's face was next to Mimi's shoulder.

"Bite me," she said through gritted teeth. It was good excuse to not have to look into Leo's piercing gaze. "Move. Please. Just harder. Make me feel it."

Leo sank her teeth into Mimi's neck in the same time as she sped up her thrusts, using her whole body to be able to fuck into Mimi harder. Her movements weren't desperate, but the calculated and confident strokes of somebody who knew exactly what they were doing.

It was infuriating and deliciously numbing. Mimi couldn't think, couldn't speak, she couldn't do anything except hold Leo closer and angle her hips upwards. She wanted Leo to take her harder, make her forget everything, make everything better.

Leo kept moving, now rubbing herself on a thigh Mimi had sneaked in between her legs. Beads of sweat was travelling from her hairline and dropping onto Mimi. *She feels so perfect.* Mimi knew she was going to come soon and fought against it. She didn't want the moment to end.

She moaned and tried to hold off, but there was no way. Not with three of Leo's long fingers stretching her so perfectly.

When Mimi came, she could have sworn that her heart was breaking. Her back arched and her nails dug into Leo's shoulders. She had orgasmed before in her life, but it had never felt like this. It had never felt like a storm of emotion that stretched from the pit of her stomach and fled through her until she felt like she was melting and freezing in the same time. Emotions threatened to flow over, and before Mimi could properly register what was happening, she had dug her face into Leo's neck and was crying her eyes out.

"What is this? Hey? Are you okay?" Leo's voice was gentle, but Mimi just shook her head against Leo's slick skin and couldn't find her voice. Her heart was breaking, and she didn't know why or how to handle it. "I'm sorry, did I hurt you? I'm so sorry, Mimi. I'm going to remove my hand, okay?"

Mimi groaned at the loss and didn't let up her hold of Leo's shoulders. She couldn't bear the thought of Leo leaving.

"What's wrong?"

Mimi sobbed but let Leo pull back so she could look at her. She looked like a wet mess but didn't have enough presence to care about that at the moment.

"It wasn't supposed to be like this." She could see the questions in Leo's eyes, but she had no answer to give. "I'm sorry."

"No, please don't be sorry. Please don't be sorry. You have nothing to be sorry for." Leo opened her arms again, and Mimi fell between them gratefully. "Let's sleep, it's late. We can talk tomorrow. I'm sorry, it's all my fault, okay? You have nothing to be sorry for." She sounded so guilty, Mimi almost corrected her but she said nothing. If she talked, she would cry. And she didn't want to cry anymore.

Instead they laid together in the silence of their room. Their bodies stuck together in certain places, and it should have been uncomfortable, but Mimi simply felt at home like this. She hugged Leo closer, listening to her heart beat. She didn't dare to think about what would happen tomorrow.

Chapter Eighteen

Leo groaned. An arm and a leg were asleep, and her skin felt sticky. She felt uncomfortable and tried to get away from the dead weight that was practically lying on top of her. Their skin stuck together as if glued and she opened her eyes. She immediately stopped struggling.

Mimi looked so peaceful lying on top of Leo's arm with her legs thrown across Leo's legs, her head resting with her mouth close to Leo's nipple.

Leo lifted her head to press a kiss on top black hair. She was still physically uncomfortable, but she could wait a little bit. Letting Mimi rest for a little bit longer and basking in the memories of last night that were coming back one after another seemed much more important than taking a shower.

After a little while, it wasn't just the stickiness of her skin and the crick in her neck that needed attention, but her bladder that made itself be known too.

"Mimi." Leo kissed the top of her head again. "Just roll over, I'll be right back."

In spite of the sleepy protest, Leo managed to roll Mimi over after a little bit of coaxing.

She went to the bathroom and took a quick shower. After also brushing her teeth, she stood still and looked at herself in the mirror for several minutes. Everything felt different, Leo felt like a new person and yet she looked the same. It didn't matter that this was the first day of her new life. She put her toothbrush down, rinsed her mouth, and then headed out of the bathroom.

Mimi was still sleeping, but as Leo walked closer her sleepy eyes opened.

"I missed you." She held out her hand. Leo let herself be pulled back onto the bed.

They kissed each other for a long time, neither of them able to get enough of each other. Eventually Leo pulled back. They needed to talk, badly, and as much as Leo had never been one for planning, this situation wasn't one she wanted to screw up. Whatever happened next, she needed to know that Mimi would be safe. Sandra and her people would be after Leo now, and she didn't want Mimi to be involved in the mess that was her life.

"We need to talk."

"Don't want to." Mimi claimed Leo's lips for another quick kiss. "Can't we just keep kissing?"

Despite the millions of reasons why not, Leo let herself be kissed for several more minutes.

*

"I don't want to go to Canada," Mimi said as Leo sat down in front of her with a loaded plate. "Not Australia either."

Leo smiled and shook her head. They were downstairs eating breakfast.

"We don't have to go anywhere."

"We have to go somewhere." Mimi dug into her scrambled eggs. "We can't hide in Gransee forever. I'm dying to go back to work, to see Paige, just go back to my life."

"I can imagine." But it was life. Leo couldn't imagine what that was like. Mimi just didn't realize that, for

155

Leo, life as she knew it was over. There was no every day to go back to. Leo sighed. There was only one thing to do. "But will you be safe in London? What if your dad tries anything like this again?"

"I'd tell Paige. The police. I could totally report them all."

"We should go our separate ways then."

Mimi pouted at the suggestion. Leo didn't know if she was happy about Mimi's obvious displeasure.

"I'm not saying you're wrong." She took another bite of food. "I just don't want to."

"Me neither," Leo said and smiled quickly. It was nice to hear that Mimi was feeling the same cautious affection that she was. "But it's still the best choice. You go back home. Just be careful, and if you see anything suspicious or feel followed, you call the police. Or even report it as soon as you're in London."

"And you?" Mimi put her fork down. She looked like her appetite was gone.

"I'll..." Leo shrugged. "I haven't worked all the kinks yet, but I'll figure it out."

"I thought not planning was your thing." Mimi pushed her plate away. There was still food on it. "I've lost my appetite. Do you want to go for a walk?"

Leo saw no reason why not.

"Sure, let's go."

*

Mimi wasn't sure why she was in such a bad mood. All she knew was that the thought of leaving Leo was making her more annoyed than the thought that her dad had had her kidnapped.

They walked slowly through Gransee, only stopping when Leo pointed something out.

"This is where I dropped an ice cream as a child, Dad got so angry because he couldn't afford to buy me a second one. Do you want to go and see the *Wartturm?* "

Mimi raised one of her eyebrows.

"The watchtower," Leo said with a smile, "it's…" Her smile faltered as her gaze fixed on something behind Mimi. "Oh, fuck."

Mimi started to turn around, but Leo grabbed her wrist, holding her in place.

"Don't turn around or they might know who you are." Fear and surprise filled Leo's face, making Mimi's heart beat faster. "They're coming for me. I don't think they are after you, but I can't be sure, so go away. There is money in my bag back at the room to pay when you check out. Go back to London, just… watch yourself."

Mimi bit her bottom lip.

"They're not going to kill you, are they?"

Leo flashed her a smile that looked equally brave and unsure.

"Of course not. Now, go."

The grip on Mimi's wrist tightened, and Leo's gaze pled to her almost desperately. *Please, Mimi.* Leo didn't have to say the words out loud, Mimi heard them anyway. They shared a final look and then Leo let go of her and kept walking. Mimi wanted to turn around and look after her but didn't dare in case the people Leo had seen were coming for her too.

Instead Mimi started walking again, tears running down her face. She turned at the next street and ran back to the bed-and-breakfast.

When she got back to their room and saw the crumpled sheets and Leo's bag standing in the corner, Mimi felt like the worst person in the word. She kept sobbing, but no more tears came. How could she have left Leo just like that? What was wrong with her?

If they hurt her I'm going to— she picked up the T-shirt she had pulled off Leo last night and put it to her face.

"Leo." She wanted to wail her name. It was crazy. *Definitely Stockholm's syndrome.* She didn't even know Leo. She didn't know Leo's full name or if Leo was really her name or something she had just said. She didn't know what Leo's favorite color was, if she had any type of higher education. Was Leo allergic to anything? Did she have any brothers or sisters? Mimi didn't know.

She picked up the clothes on the floor and stuffed them inside Leo's bag. Once everything was packed she put the bag on her shoulder.

There were a lot of things she didn't know about Leo, but one thing was perfectly clear. Mimi had to make sure she was safe. One way or another.

Chapter Nineteen

There were many things Mimi was, but stupid wasn't one of them. Usually scared wasn't one either. But she had to admit that she felt slightly nervous as she made her way toward the train station on her own. She walked with determination, refusing to stop for anything or anyone. She tried to ignore the small voice of fear in her head. *What if they are looking for you too?*

She finally reached the station, located the ticket booth, and went up to the woman sitting there.

"One ticket to Berlin, please." She hoped that the woman spoke at least a little bit English.

"6.80 euros, please."

"When is the next train?"

The answer was presented with such a thick German accent that Mimi, at first, didn't understand, but when the clerk repeated the time, she nodded in understanding. She said thank you, opened Leo's bag, and rummaged for money.

Once she had paid, she waited for the clerk to point her in the direction of the train and then she set off, grateful that she would be able to catch the train that was leaving in just a few minutes. She was happy that she didn't have to wait for too long. Better enter her dad's office like a raging tornado than a tired little girl who had spent half the day waiting for trains.

The train came and Mimi got in. Sat down. Fixed her gaze on the view outside. If she had had a phone she would have called Paige. Her only friend deserved to know what had happened to her. But was Paige really her only friend? Mimi groaned and fought back against the tears that never seemed far away anymore. Travelling by train had been so much more fun when she had had Leo by her side.

She wanted the train to hurry up. Go faster. She needed to save Leo.

*

A little bit less than two hours later, Mimi found herself outside her dad's building. It was his office—she didn't actually know where he lived—but this was the address where Leo was supposed to drop her off before. So Mimi guessed and hoped it was where she would find him. The worry she had felt earlier had abated now, and except for the stressed beating of her heart, she felt calm. *You have the weapon,* she reminded herself, *just threaten to go to the police.* She looked at her face in the reflective glass by the door. There were black lines under her eyes, and her cheeks were a little bit hollow, but at least she looked very pissed off. *Good.* She needed that fire in her eyes when she faced the only man who had ever been able to tell her what to do.

She rang the bell. It sounded unnaturally loud and did nothing to calm her buried nerves. She chewed on her bottom lip as she waited, but quickly composed herself when she heard steps on the other side.

"Yes?" Mimi looked at the young man on the other side, short with brown hair and glasses. She didn't know him, and guessed he worked for her dad.

"I'm here to see Mr. Adam."

"Very well." He stepped aside to let her through the door. "Who should I say is here to see him?"

"His daughter." She sat down on a chair in the room he had led her to, acting like she owned the place.

She smiled triumphantly. Her dad had thought she would return humbled and scared, instead she was there completely on her own terms. She still had the power, and nothing meant as much to Mimi as the feeling of being in power. She rolled her shoulders, trying to relax completely while the man went to get the man of the house.

"Who?"

Mimi couldn't help but giggle. Her dad sounded equally surprised and furious. As his steps got closer, she got up from the chair so she could greet him standing up.

When he appeared in the doorway, the sight of his thin and tall frame caused her to shiver a little bit. *I'm an adult now,* she told herself, *and the bastard had you kidnapped. Be brave. For Leo.* With Leo firmly on her mind, she smiled sweetly.

"Hi, Dad. Aren't you happy to see me?"

Her dad produced a strained smile that didn't reach his eyes.

"Of course I am." He opened his arms as if wanting to hug her. "I'm just surprised. You were kidnapped! I assumed—"

She put a hand to his chest before he could envelop her in an embrace.

"Let me stop you right there." She fixed her gaze on him. "*You* had me kidnapped. And I know that Sandra Sousa helped you."

His mouth dropped open.

"You thought I wouldn't find out? I've outsmarted you." She grinned. "Your good-for-nothing-run-away daughter found out and got away from her kidnapper." That part wasn't completely true, but Mimi didn't want to get Leo into more trouble that was necessary.

Her dad just stared at her, clearly at loss for words. "What?"

"Where is Mother?" Mimi looked behind him. "Does she know about this?" She started to walk towards the doorway where her dad had appeared. She wanted to find her mother.

"She doesn't know. She's with her personal trainer in Nice."

"With her personal trainer in..." Mimi sighed. "Can we be more of a stereotype?" She fell down on the chair, clutching Leo's bag in her right hand.

"So what's your plan now?" She looked up at him. "I'm here. You got me. What was your plan now?"

Her dad sat down on the sofa next to her.

"Now you come to your senses and stay here." His voice was void of any emotion. "You should be grateful for the protection we're offering you. The protection we've always given you." He pursed his lips. "Don't you think I know how you live? That little business of yours is barely keeping you on your feet. How much longer until it won't? Then you'll come running back to us. We just wanted to hurry you up a bit."

"You're actually insane." Mimi folded her arms over her chest. She shook her head. "What protection is that? Locking me in the basement when I did something you don't like? Forcing relationships I don't want on me? Not wanting me to have a life of my own? Wanting me to..." *be some kind of Mandy clone.* But even in this moment she couldn't mention her sister. Her perfect sister.

"Kazumi!" Her dad practically yelled to interrupt her. "You are my daughter, there are certain obligations you have to meet, one of them is not running away."

"I wanted to be free."

"None of us are free!" He really was yelling now, and despite Mimi's resolve to not show fear, she couldn't help but lean backwards, her heart pounding. "Do you think I had a choice when I was young? My dad was much harsher than I ever was with you. I was expected to take over the business, I was supposed to get married and have children. I expect the same from my children. This isn't strange or impossible request."

"It is an impossible request. It has always been an impossible request. I can't be what you want me to be."

They stared at each other in anger, neither of them willing to give even an inch to the other. That was the curse, Mimi mused, of being his daughter. They were too alike, but with some very crucial differences.

"I was assured you would come to no harm," her dad said after a few moments of silence. "They were supposed to keep you for a few days, scare you. Then take you home. To us."

"Oh, I got scared, Dad." Mimi swallowed. "I've been hit, locked inside the trunk of a moving car, and for several days I was so drugged I have no memories of what happened."

Her dad twitched and one of his hands gripped the arm of the chair.

"I'm going to call Sandra and give her a piece of my mind."

He looked determined, as if he was planning to go and call her right away. Mimi clutched Leo's bag tighter. She didn't want to fold. She didn't want to forgive. She didn't want to utter the words that she was planning to utter. But she needed to. *For Leo, remember?* Leo with the sad eyes and the crooked smile and the kisses that rocked Mimi's world.

"Dad." She forced her voice to sound friendly rather than angry. "You don't have to kidnap me to get me to listen to you. I don't want you to kidnap me in order to manipulate my feelings toward you and Mother. You could go to jail."

"What proof do you have?" He looked unsure.

"I was gone for a whole week, Dad! I have bruises. My car is gone."

He crossed his arms over his chest.

"All circumstantial. And I doubt you could afford a lawyer." He shook his head.

Mimi reveled in the hate she felt. Hate for the man in front of her. *I will never forget. I will never forgive.*

"Would you risk it? *You* kidnapped me. You did this. If I wanted, I could go to the police right now." The threats were right there, on the tip of her tongue. "You could go to jail, Dad." She smiled widely. "Mom too, maybe. Or maybe I could sue you." His shoulders twitched at that. "Take all your fortune to fund that 'little business of mine.' Guess how many sparkly dresses I could make out of all your stocks and bonds? And even if I didn't win in court, could you really survive the media scandal?" She wanted to laugh but was satisfied with just a mirthless smile. She felt stone cold inside.

Her dad's eyes were wide and his mouth was slightly open. His chest heaved. "I know what I did was desperate, but it was a tough situation." Even the tone of his voice was disgustingly hopeful. "What can we do to move

past here? There must be something I can do so we can…."
He breathed deeply. "What do you want?"

"To be left alone, first of all."

She didn't know how long that promise would last,
but her second request was currently more important.

I'm coming, Leo.

Chapter Twenty

Leo hit the floor. *You idiot.* Her mouth was full of warm salty liquid, and her cheek was no longer hurting but rather burning after being punched so many times. *You stupid, stupid woman. Sandra knows how much you love Gransee. Of course she would search for you there.*

She tried to fight back as two large hands grabbed her shoulders and pulled her to her feet. She had no strength left. All she could do was groan and hope it would all be over soon. *You're truly an idiot. You should have known what would happen if you ever crossed Sandra.*

Something, not a hand, was slapped across her face, and she fell back to the floor, hitting the back of her head in the process. Her ears were ringing, and when she opened her eyes she couldn't focus her gaze on anything. She closed them again, not wanting to face the blurry red mess.

Faces flashed in front of her. Sandra's. Her dad's. *Mimi's.* Mimi smiling, safe somewhere far away. Leo groaned. She tried to get up and failed. Her arms didn't have enough energy to push her off the floor.

The boot came out of nowhere and hit her hard in the abdomen. *Please.* She would have called out, but her mouth couldn't form any words. Her whole face was swollen. She tried to shield herself, but the kicks kept coming. There was nothing she could do to protect herself. *Helpless idiot.*

She forced her eyes to open just in time to see the boot-clad foot coming right toward her head. She closed her eyes again and waited for the incoming blow. When it did, the dark came for her.

*

"Poor baby."

At first Leo thought she had imagined the words, that Sandra had somehow made it into a dream that had been somewhat pleasant at first. Slowly she returned to reality and noticed that her body hurt in a way she had never experienced before. She tried to take a deep breath, but all that followed was a shallow stream of air and a wheezing in her chest. Her head pounded as she tried to open her eyes. Only one of them opened. The other one was covered with red.

"Poor little Leo-baby." Sandra was standing by her bed, a cruel smile on her lips. *"Are you trying to say something, sweetness?"*

She giggled softly and traced the line of Leo's eyebrow. Leo tried to move her head but just winced in pain.

"Please," she croaked. In English.

Sandra giggled again.

"Did I beat the French out of you? That's definitely new."

A phone rang, the touch on her eyebrow disappeared. She felt more than heard Sandra get up from the bed. She regarded Sandra with her one good eye.

"Oui, allô." Sandra's eyes widened, then she switched to English. "Oh, hi, I'm so happy that... what?" She smiled cruelly at Leo. "Oh, I'm sorry, but your call is

too late. She has already been taken care of. We were just about to get rid of the body."

Cold fear attacked Leo and with the last strength, strength she possibly couldn't have, she shouted at the top of her lungs.

"No! She's lying! I'm alive. I'm alive." *I'm alive.* She closed her mouth. She was still alive. But for how long she didn't know.

Sandra's face turned to stone. "Yes, I see." She said into the phone. "Alright, I will do as you say. But you and I need to have a word about this. I'm not going down just because you chickened out."

Leo closed her eye again. Her vision was so blurry it was making her headache worse.

She listened as Sandra said bye and swore loudly in French. Then the bed dipped as Leo was joined on it again. A hand landed on top of Leo's already aching arm and squeezed, making a whimper escape her throat.

"I don't know how you pulled this off." Sandra's voice was low, poisonous. *"And don't think I will forget it."*

"I don't know..." Gasp *"...what you are talking about!"* Leo hissed through gritted teeth.

"Whatever you say." Sandra stood up again. *"We better not meet again, sweetness. One of us won't survive it."*

Leo listened to her receding steps, then she fell unconscious again. *I'm alive.*

*

"Let me see her."

Leo opened her eyes again. She noticed to her relief that this time she could open both of them. She also noticed that she had been moved. She didn't recognize the light blue wallpaper or the subtle scent of disinfectant. Was she in a hospital?

"Miss, I don't think—"

"Just try and stop me!"

Was that Mimi's voice?

It still hurt to move her head, but Leo managed to turn to the side just in time to see the door spring open and Mimi walk through it.

Mimi looked different than Leo remembered. Less scared and tired. There was color back in her cheeks, and her hair was falling down her back in black locks. She wasn't wearing make-up from what Leo could see, but the hand that came up to cradle her cheek definitely sported professionally manicured nails.

"Hi." Mimi's eyes were tender when they looked at her. "How are you feeling? I'm so sorry I couldn't get to you sooner."

"I don't know." Leo still sounded strange, to her annoyance. She grimaced. "Could I have some water?"

"Oh, of course." Mimi left her side only to come back moments later with a small cup. "Here." She helped Leo lift her head and put the cup to her lips.

The water felt divine, the cool stream soothing her mouth and throat. But the feeling of being a helpless child was less divine.

"Thank you," she said when Mimi took the cup away.

"Any time."

They looked at each other awkwardly.

"What happened?" Leo had to ask.

Mimi stroked some hairs off of her forehead, looking like she couldn't believe Leo was actually there in front of her.

"I asked my dad for help." Their eyes met. "It's okay. He owes me now if he doesn't want me to run to the police. I just promised to not report him."

"But..." Leo tried to sit up, but Mimi pushed her back down.

"Don't sit up. You need rest, you idiot." Leo let herself be pushed back with another grimace. "He called Sandra and threatened to expose her business if she didn't let you go unharmed. I'm sorry we were late." She trailed her fingers down something on Leo's cheek. It must have been a big bruise, because even Mimi's gentle touch hurt. She whimpered pathetically and Mimi removed her hand.

"I'm so sorry," she said in a low voice, then she smiled a teasing smile. "How are you going to kidnap anyone in this state?"

Leo tried to return the smile, but the side of her mouth hurt too much.

"Anyways." Mimi sighed. "I got dad's driver to drive me to the location where Sandra had been keeping you. I found you on a dirty mattress on the floor all beaten up." She produced a sound somewhere between a sob and a hiccup. "I called an ambulance, they brought you here."

"You went by yourself?" Leo couldn't believe her ears.

Mimi made an impatient gesture.

"I had my dad's driver with me. And besides, Sandra had already said she would leave you there for us to pick up."

Leo tried to swallow which made her cough.

"How long have I been here?"

"About a day, I had to go to my dad's and change clothes." Mimi's eyes filled with emotion. "And as bad as you looked, the doctor assured me that you weren't as close to death as I thought." She closed her eyes and moved her face so Leo couldn't see them. "I was worried." She brought a hand up to her face as to wipe off a stray tear.

"When can I leave?"

"I don't know. You have a concussion, a couple of badly bruised ribs, and a broken arm. I'm quite sure they'll at least want to keep you overnight, maybe longer."

"Nothing worse?" Leo felt pleasantly surprised.

"Nope. Before you know it you'll be up and walking like nothing ever happened."

Silence fell between them, both of them knowing that neither of them could ever act like nothing had ever happened.

"Tell me the truth," Leo said. "What did Sandra say? Is she going to come after me?"

"I hope not." Mimi grabbed her hand gently. "I had dad promise that if she did, he'd expose her, should it be ten years into the future. You're free to do what you want. Well, perhaps not work for her." Mimi lowered her voice. "That part of your life might be over now, sorry about that."

"Don't be sorry. I'm not. And it's not your fault," Leo hurried to answer. "None of this was your fault. I need you to know that." She really did need Mimi to know that. It didn't matter that Mimi had been a pain in the ass, she had been a victim. Leo was the one who had—

"It's hard to tell yourself that when the person you like is lying broken in front of you." Mimi's smile was sad. "I didn't want you to get hurt. Not in the end anyway."

"Will you stay?" Leo tried to reach for her. "Will you stay until I'm released?" She didn't care if she sounded pathetic or weak, she just wanted Mimi to stay with her. She didn't want them to go their separate ways, not yet. She needed a few more minutes of Mimi's spitfire eyes and expressive smile.

"I'm sorry." Mimi looked reluctant.

"No, don't be. I understand, you need to get back to your work." Leo looked to the side.

"That's not it." Mimi squeezed Leo's hand. "I would love to stay, but I shouldn't. I'm eager to leave Germany. I need to get back to my store."

A thought entered Leo's mind.

"What did you have to agree to in order to save me?"

"Pfft." Mimi shook her head. "As long as I don't go the police, he will do anything. He has no claim on me."

"He might go after you again."

"Maybe. And Sandra might go after you." Mimi straightened up and removed her hand from Leo's. "Well," she said. "It is what it is. I have to get going. Your medical bills have been taken care of."

She stood up. Leo didn't know what to say, and apparently neither did Mimi. They looked at each other. A whole array of different emotions played on Mimi's face. She leaned down and pressed her lips against Leo's in a quick, chaste kiss.

"In my mind, I believe that you saved me," she whispered against Leo's lips. "And for that I will always be grateful."

Leo didn't know what to reply so she said nothing, just nodded and tried smiling again.

"Oh, I almost forgot." Mimi placed Leo's worn leather bag on the foot of the bed. "Here is your bag, I put something extra in there for you to discover later." She tweaked Leo's toes under the cover. "Bye!" With that she was gone.

Leo sat up straight and reached for the bag in spite of the pain. She couldn't wait. She opened it. Everything seemed to be there, including an extra envelope full of what looked like a lot of cash and a small postcard. She didn't flip through the money and instead looked at the postcard. She looked at the picture of a small nightingale with the words *Willkommen in Gransee* written over it. She flipped it over and read Mimi's short text.

> *Kidnapping review*
> *10/10 for effort. 2/10 for execution. 7/10 for food. 10/10 for lovemaking skills.*
> *Don't you dare forget me.*
> *xoxo, Mimi.*

Leo clutched the postcard to her chest and burst out laughing. It didn't matter how much it hurt, she didn't stop laughing until tears were streaming down her face.

*

Mimi hurried out of the hospital and to the taxi that waited for her there. As soon as she was safe inside it and on the way to the airport, she took out her brand new phone, another 'gift' from her dad. She dialed the only number she knew by heart.

"Paige? It's me. It's Mimi. Yes, I'm okay." Tears started falling down her cheeks. She sobbed. "I'm alive. I'm okay." *I'm alive.*

Chapter Twenty-One

One month later…

"This is your resume?"

Leo felt her face heat. She was thirty-two and didn't have much she could actually put on her resume. Which is why this was no less than the fifteenth interview she had been to since settling in London two weeks ago. She had been staying at a hostel, but she really needed a job. Eventually even her moderate savings would run out.

She needed a job.

"I know it's not very impressive," she tried and played her only trump card. "But I speak German, French, Turkish, and English. I doubt you can find many other people who can do that."

"Turkish, you say?" The man looked at her resume again. "The other languages aren't hard to find."

Well, fine then, old man, Leo thought, but she just smiled as politely as she could. *Please like me. Please hire me.*

"We do have one Turkish company that we trade with." He produced a sound somewhere between a sigh and a cough. "I'll be in touch."

She got up.

"Miss? Maybe you should just apply as a translator. It won't pay that much anymore, but there are plenty of companies that want freelance translators for instruction manuals, television series, et cetera. Use your language in that way. It won't make a career but…." He shrugged. Leo got the message.

"Thank you for the advice." She shook his hand and exited the office. She left the door open. He could get up and close it himself.

When she was outside she got on the second hand bike that she had bought last week. It was an old, probably dangerous thing, but it was good enough for now. It got her from point A to point B quite comfortably and, depending on where, sometimes faster than the tube. It was also cheaper than the tube.

She cycled down to the Thames and bought a hot dog from a vendor that stood there. She looked at the flowing water underneath and sighed. *I should have known better than to apply for a job in central London.* Maybe she should just forget about trying to get a "real" job and look at translating things like the man had suggested. *It was better than nothing.*

*

Mimi ran from the tube to her front door. It had started to drizzle, and even if it was summer rain and not the downpour London was famous for, she didn't feel like getting wet. She cradled her bag with the money from today's business as she went up the stairs and got inside her apartment.

Before pulling off her drape jacket, she went up to a safe she had inside one of the cabinets over the sink. She took out an envelope containing today's earnings and put it inside. It wasn't much, but Mimi had started to hope. Maybe everything would be okay after all.

She had taken both her shoes and jacket off when there was a knock on the door. Mimi raised an eyebrow.

Who in this day and age visited someone without calling first?

Whoever it was, they knocked again. Mimi took a few slow steps toward the door. She didn't like the unknown. Not when it came knocking at the door. Not since—

"Mimi?"

Mimi's heart froze like a lake in winter. She knew that voice. But it couldn't be. At first she got scared. Why would Leo come looking for her? Had she followed her home? Mimi shook her head. *She already knows where you live, stupid. She wouldn't need to follow you home.* Time seemed to slow down as Mimi stared at her door in panic. If Leo wasn't there to hurt her, why was she there? *It's Leo.* Time sped up again as Mimi remembered. Leo's smile. Leo's smell. The hurt look in Leo's eyes. Leo's kiss. Leo broken and alone, abandoned, on a hospital bed in Germany. *Leo.*

Mimi couldn't move fast enough. She leapt to the door, struggling to open the two locks.

"Hang on," she called out, scared that Leo would give up and leave. Her fingers wouldn't obey fast enough.

She finally got the locks open and pulled on the handle hard. The door flew open and a very surprised looking Leo peeked inside. They stared at each other, both of them blinking like deer in headlights.

Leo looked good. There were no signs of bruises or the black eye she had had last time they met. Instead she looked better than Mimi could ever remember seeing her. Despite sitting on the stairs, she looked elegant in a pair of black jeans and a blue shirt with a beige jacket on top.

Mimi didn't know what to say, so she just stared. *Do I hug her? Why is she here? Do I hug her?*

When Mimi still hadn't said anything for a long time, Leo looked pained.

"I'm sorry," she said. "I shouldn't have come." She put her palms up. "I'll go, I'm… sorry." She started to turn away and Mimi grabbed a hold of her arm, stopping her.

"Don't be silly." She let go as soon as Leo stopped turning. She folded hair arms over her chest. "Come inside."

They walked into her flat. It was messy, like usual, but that seemed so unimportant.

"Tea?"

"Um… sure."

Mimi kept her back to Leo as she went over to her kitchenette and turned the kettle on. "Just sit down by the table." There was a thud behind her, a familiar creaking coming from her old wooden chairs. *What do I do?* The situation was strange. Awkward.

She took out her tea box and placed it in front of Leo. "Choose." When Leo started flipping through the different teas, Mimi kept her eyes on her. Leo looked wrong, placed there in her kitchen, too big for her little apartment. Too big for her world.

Leo held up a teabag. "Lavender-liquorice, that can't be good, can it?"

"It's not as good as cinnamon-liquorice, but it's okay." Mimi looked on as Leo once again flipped through the different kinds of teas, eventually she lost her patience and pulled the box away from her. "How about I just choose, okay? Something normal." She took out two bags of peppermint-three-ways and prepared two cups by the counter.

"Thanks," Leo said, "you have way too many kinds of tea."

"I like having a choice." Mimi sat down at the table too and placed the cups on the table. Silence fell between them as they awkwardly stared at the steaming cups.

"I wanted to see you," Leo said after a little while. "I don't know if it was appropriate or allowed by your dad or…"

"I do whatever I want," Mimi hurried to say, "my dad can't hurt me anymore."

"Really? I find that hard to believe." Their gazes locked again, but Mimi hurried to look away. She couldn't look at Leo and not be transported back. Back to France. Back to Germany. Back to the nightmare.

"No." She giggled at the memory. "The last time I saw him, I threatened to go to the police. He said I don't have any proof and it would be my word against his."

Leo's eyebrows knotted and she leaned forward.

"He is right."

"He is full of shit." Mimi shook her head. "What about my bruises? I took photos when I got home. I told Paige every detail I could remember. And even if I had no proof? I doubt he could risk the scandal if I went to the media."

Leo looked uncomfortable at the mention of Mimi's bruises.

"I'm glad everything worked out for you."

"I always get my way," Mimi said with a smile. "What about you? Sandra isn't giving you trouble, is she?"

"No." Leo shook her head. "She actually called me."

"She didn't!" Mimi took a careful sip of her hot tea.

"She threatened me." Leo took a hold of the thread from the teabag and stirred it around in the cup. "She told me that if she goes down, I go down with her, so I better keep my mouth shut. More or less."

"Are you scared?"

Leo shrugged.

"I've been a criminal for all of my adult life, being scared of the police is nothing new. I'm more scared of not managing to make myself a life. A proper life."

*

"A proper life?" Leo didn't like Mimi's question. She didn't want to admit to being a total loser. Which was what she felt like.

"I want a job." She said. "A proper job with honest pay." She focused on her tea again, but it was still too hot to drink. How Mimi had managed to drink half already was beyond her. "But it isn't so easy to get one when you're thirty-two with an empty resume."

"Is it completely empty?"

Leo grimaced.

"I didn't know if I should put my summer working as a youth leader at a camp when I was seventeen."

"Youth leader, really?" Mimi chuckled, but it sounded forced. She seemed to have trouble meeting Leo's gaze which made Leo worried. "Can't you just lie?"

"I have no references."

"I can lie for you if you want." Mimi looked at her then. "You should get a second chance, doesn't matter your age."

"That's sweet of you, but I think I'm going to see if I can become a translator of some sorts. For instruction manuals or anything. Might as well use all the languages I have."

"That's a good idea." Mimi's cup seemed to be empty. "I can't believe we're sitting here. You and I."

"I know what you mean." It did feel very strange. It was hard to believe everything they had gone through had happened just last month and not a decade ago. It was hard to believe that Mimi was sitting in front of her, alive and well, when it hadn't been even two months since Leo had held her down, drugged her, locked her in a trunk. Leo racked her brain. *I never hit her, did I?* She didn't think she could bear it if she had. She swallowed back a sudden wave of nausea.

"I am so, so, sorry."

Mimi's eyes went very wide. Leo didn't want to talk about it either. She didn't want to mention the elephant in the room. But if she ever wanted to move forward, she needed to talk. *They* needed to talk.

"I don't want your apology." Mimi's tone of voice had developed an edge. The next words uttered just sounded tired. "I don't want to talk about it."

"We have to." Leo's heart broke. "We have to. I want… I want us to be friends. And to be friends we need to acknowledge what happened."

"I forgive you, okay?" Mimi pushed away from the table and pursed her lips. "Is that what you need?"

"I'm not looking for forgiveness." Leo waited until Mimi looked at her again. "I need to know that you're okay. I need to know that you don't… have nightmares. I need to know that I don't star in any nightmares you might have."

Mimi looked at her then. She reached forward and waited until Leo put her hand forward.

"I have nightmares." She said in a small voice. "A lot of them. Every night. Supposedly it's natural. Sometimes you're there." When Leo wanted to pull her hand from Mimi's grip, Mimi held on tighter. "Sometimes I can't get to you. Sometimes people hurt you. Sometimes people hurt both of us. In my dreams you never hurt me."

Leo felt relief wash over her even if she couldn't believe it at first.

"We can't just forget about it." She forced the words out. "It happened. I hurt you."

"You did." Mimi gave her hand a final squeeze and then let go. "And that wasn't okay. But I want to move on. I hope you can respect that."

Leo nodded. "Well, it's late." She had forgotten why she had wanted to come there in the first place. What did she want? A date? Who was she kidding? She got up. "I should let you sleep."

"It's seven-thirty," Mimi called after her. "Don't leave yet."

"Why should I stay?" Leo had barely turned around before Mimi was there, pressing their lips together. Blood rushed through her veins, heart sped up and throat dried. She barely dared to move, scared to do the wrong thing, scared to scare Mimi away.

"That's why you should stay." Mimi sounded like she was about to start crying. "For this." She touched a finger to Leo's chest, over her heart. "Because you want to. Because I want you to."

Leo licked her lips, wanting to kiss Mimi again. Crazy, brave little spitfire. Who had endured so much. There was so much Leo wanted to know about her. Almost more than the amount she wanted to keep her safe.

"Where do you propose we go from here, then?" Leo's voice was husky. She wondered if Mimi could hear the loud pounding of her heart.

"I propose we order dinner. Pizza maybe." Leo grinned and Mimi smiled triumphantly. "After that we talk more. Then we go to bed, to sleep. I am a lady after all." She winked. "Then tomorrow, you go home to wherever you live. We have exchanged numbers so we both dance around in awkwardness on who will call who first, and do we wait three days, or do we call right away."

"And then?" Mimi was amazing. And funny. Leo couldn't stop looking at her.

"And then?" Mimi bit her lip. "Then maybe we date." An adorable blush spread across her cheeks. "If we feel like it after all this trouble."

"We'll wait and see then."

"So… food?" Mimi held up her phone. "I know this place that does pizza for four pounds. We'll have to go and pick it up though. They don't deliver."

"Sure."

"Sit down on the sofa." Mimi pointed at something that probably was a sofa under several rolls of fabric. "You can move the pile of fabrics. Just push them to the side."

Leo moved them carefully, despite what Mimi had said. She was itching to ask how Mimi's business was doing, but since Mimi was currently on the phone with the pizzeria, Leo stayed quiet.

"The pizza sucks though," Mimi said when she got off the phone. "But at least it's cheap food. I didn't feel like serving you ramen, my usual Thursday night feast."

"It would have been fine. Mimi, how is your sho—"

"Leo." Mimi interrupted, her facial expression stern. Whatever she was about to ask was probably quite important. Leo waited.

"Yes?" Her hands shook.

"What is your last name?" Mimi leaned forward.

Leo laughed.

About the Author

Kathy grew up travelling around the world but is now settled with her wife in Sweden. By day she is a primary school teacher, by night, a writer, and with the little spare time she has left she enjoys cooking, playing video games and spending time with her family.

Other Titles Available From
Triplicity Publishing

Worlds Apart by S.L. Gape. Hollywood A-lister Heidi Spencer-Brady is everything you'd expect of an Idol. Loved by all, the British Beauty is graceful, talented, humble and so far removed from the 'typical' LA scene. When her husband's infidelity with his new 'leading lady' is leaked, Dawn, Heidi's best friend and manager, goes all out to protect her. She arranges for Heidi to go back to the UK and stay on her cousins farm they had visited as children, much to the disappointment of the animal fearing Heidi.

Castor Valley (Law & Order Series Book 2) by Graysen Morgen. Jessie Henry is torn when she reads about the capture of the Doyle brothers, two young men who were part of her old gang. Unable to let them hang for a crime she's sure they didn't commit, Jessie leaves her wife and the Town of Boone Creek behind, and sets out on a journey back to the one place she thought she'd never see again, *Castor Valley*. Ellie Henry watches the love of her life leave, not knowing if she will ever return. When she gets an odd telegram, nearly a week later, she fears Jessie is in trouble. With no other choice, she goes to the one person who can help her.

Close Enough to Touch by Cade Brogan. Joanna Grey injects the deadly poison into the chamber of the syringe— time after time. She's murdered before and she'll do it again. She's intelligent, educated, and beautiful. Rylee Hayes is a respected homicide detective. Her best friends are her grandparents, her coonhound, and her partner—in that order. Kenzie Bigham is the single mom of a thirteen-year-old, a church secretary, and a woman who's struggled much of her adult life with her own sexuality. Their paths will cross when Rylee's new investigation involves members of Kenzie's congregation. Will Rylee have what it takes to meet the challenge of a serial killer who's proven herself to be a more than worthy opponent?

Fight to the Top by S. L. Gape. Georgia is a forty year old, single, Area Director from Manchester, UK who is all work and definitely no play. Having no time to socialise or spend time with her family she prides herself on being fit and well-polished. Erika is an Area Director for the same company, but in the United States. Whilst she is concentrating so heavily on the promotion she has been fighting for, she's starting to feel like her life outside of work is falling apart. The two women are exceptionally different, and worlds apart. Both of their lives are turned upside down when their jobs are snatched from under their noses, and they are suddenly faced with being thrown together by their bosses for one last major project...in Texas.

***Boone Creek (Law & Order Series book 1*)** by Graysen Morgen. Jessie Henry is looking for a new life. She's unknown in the town of Boone Creek when she arrives, and wants to keep it that way. When she's offered the job of Town Marshal, she takes it, believing that protecting others and upholding the law is the penance for her past. Ellie Fray is a widowed, shopkeeper. She generally keeps to herself, but the mysterious new Town Marshal both intrigues and infuriates her. She believes the last thing the town needs is someone stirring up trouble with the outlaws who have taken over.

Witness by Joan L. Anderson. Becca and Kate have lived together for eight years, and have always spent their vacation in a tropical paradise, lying on a beach. This year, Becca wanted to try something different: a seven day, 65-mile hike in the beautiful Cascade Mountains of Washington state. Their peaceful vacation turns to horror when they stumble upon a brutal murder taking place in the back country.

Too Soon by S.L. Gape. Brooke is a twenty-nine year old detective from Oxford, who has her life pretty much planned out until her boss and partner of nine years, Maria, tells her their relationship is over. When Brooke finds out the truth, that Maria cheated on her with their best friend Paula, she decides to get her life back on track by getting away for six weeks in Anglesey, North Wales. Chloe, a thirty three year old artist and art director, owns a log cabin on Anglesey where she spends each weekend painting and surfing. After returning from a surf, she stumbles upon the somewhat uptight and enigmatic Brooke.

Blue Ice Landing by KA Moll. Coy is a beautiful blonde with a southern accent and a successful practice as a physician assistant. She has a comfortable home, good friends, and a loving family. She's also a widow, carrying a burden of responsibility for her wife's untimely death. Coby is a woman with secrets. She's estranged from her family, a recovering alcoholic, and alone because she's convinced that she's unlovable. When she loses her job as a heavy equipment operator, she'll accept one that'll force her to step way outside her comfort zone. When Coy quits her job to accept a position in Antarctica, her path will cross with Coby's. Their attraction to one another will be immediate, and despite their differences, it won't be long before they fall in love. But for these two, with all their baggage, will love be enough?

Never Quit (Never Series book 2) by Graysen Morgen. Two years after stepping away from the action as a Coast Guard Rescue Swimmer to become an instructor, Finley finds herself in charge of the most difficult class of cadets she's ever faced, while also juggling the taxing demands of having a home life with her partner Nicole, and their fifteen year old daughter. Jordy Ross gave up everything, dropping out of college, and leaving her family behind, to join the Coast Guard and become a rescue swimmer cadet. The extreme training tests her fitness level, pushing her mentally and physically further than she's ever been in her life, but it's the aggressive competition between her and another female cadet that proves to be the most challenging.

For a Moment's Indiscretion by KA Moll. With ten years of marriage under their belt, Zane and Jaina are coasting. The little things they used to do for one another have fallen by the wayside. They've gotten busy with life. They've forgotten to nurture their love and relationship. Even soul mates can stumble on hard times and have marital difficulties. Enter Amelia, a new faculty member in Jaina's building. She's new in town, young, and very pretty. When an argument with Zane causes Jaina to storm out angry, she reaches out to Amelia. Of course, she seizes the opportunity. And for a moment of indiscretion, Jaina could lose everything.

Never Let Go (Never Series book 1) by Graysen Morgen. For Coast Guard Rescue Swimmer, Finley Morris, life is good. She loves her job, is well respected by her peers, and has been given an opportunity to take her career to the next level. The only thing missing is the love of her life, who walked out, taking their daughter with her, seven years earlier. When Finley gets a call from her ex, saying their teenage daughter is coming to spend the summer with her, she's floored. While spending more time with her daughter, whom she doesn't get to see often, and learning to be a full-time parent, Finley quickly realizes she has not, and will never, let go of what is important.

Pursuit by Joan L. Anderson. Claire is a workaholic attorney who flies to Paris to lick her wounds after being dumped by her girlfriend of seventeen years. On the plane she chats with the young woman sitting next to her, and when they land the woman is inexplicably detained in Customs. Claire is surprised when she later runs into the woman in the city. They agree to meet for breakfast the next morning, but when the woman doesn't show up Claire goes to her hotel and makes a horrifying discovery. She soon finds herself ensnared in a web of intrigue and international terrorism, becoming the target of a high stakes game of cat and mouse through the streets of Paris.

Wrecked by Sydney Canyon. To most people, the *Duchess* is a myth formed by old pirates tales, but to Reid Cavanaugh, a Caribbean island bum and one of the best divers and treasure hunters in the world, it's a real, seventeenth century pirate ship—the holy grail of underwater treasure hunting. Reid uses the same cunning tactics she always has before setting out to find the lost ship. However, she is forced to bring her business partner's daughter along as collateral this time because he doesn't trust her. Neither woman is thrilled, but being cooped up on a small dive boat for days, forces them to get know each other quickly.

Arson by Austen Thorne. Madison Drake is a detective for the Stetson Beach Police Department. The last thing she wants to do is show a new detective the ropes, especially when a fire investigation becomes arson to cover up a murder. Madison butts heads with Tara, her trainee, deals with sarcasm from Nic, her ex-girlfriend who is a patrol officer, and finds calm in the chaos of police work with Jamie, her best friend who is the county medical examiner. Arson is the first of many in a series of novella episodes surrounding the fictional Stetson Beach Police Department and Detective Madison Drake.

Change of Heart by KA Moll. Courtney Holloman is a woman at the top of her game. She's successful, wealthy, and a highly sought after Washington lobbyist. She has money, her job, booze, and nothing else. In quiet moments, against her will, her mind drifts back to her days in high school and to all that she gave up. Jack Camdon is a complex woman, and yet not at all. She is also a woman who has never moved beyond the sudden and unexplained departure of her high school sweetheart, her lover, and her soul mate. When circumstances bring Courtney back to town two decades later, their paths will cross. Will it be too late?

***Mommies (Bridal Series book 3)* by Graysen Morgen.** Britton and her wife Daphne have been married for a year and a half and are happy with their life, until Britton's mother hounds her to find out why her sister Bridget hasn't decided to have children yet. This prompts Daphne to bring up the big subject of having kids of their own with Britton. Britton hadn't really thought much about having kids, but her love for Daphne makes her see life and their future together in a whole new way when they decide to become mommies.

***Haunting Love* by K.A. Moll.** Anna Crestwood was raised in the strict beliefs of a religious sect nestled in the foothills of the Smoky Mountains. She's a lesbian with a ton of baggage—fearful, guilty, and alone. Very few things would compel her to leave the familiar. The job offer of a lifetime is one of them. Gabe Garst is a police officer. She's also a powerful medium. Her work with juvenile delinquents and ghosts is all that keeps her going. Inside she's dead, certain that her capacity to love is buried six feet under. Anna and Gabe's paths cross. Their attraction is immediate, but they hold back until all hope seems lost.

***Rapture & Rogue* by Sydney Canyon.** Taren Rauley is happy and in a good relationship, until the one person she thought she'd never see again comes back into her life. She struggles to keep the past from colliding with the present as old feelings she thought were dead and gone, begin to haunt her. In college, Gianna Revisi was a mastermind, ring-leading, crime boss. Now, she has a great life and spends her time running Rapture and Rogue, the two establishments she built from the ground up. The last person she ever expects to see walk into one of them, is the girl who walked out on her, breaking her heart five years ago.

Second Chance by Sydney Canyon. After an attack on her convoy, Marine Corps Staff Sergeant, Darien Hollister, must learn to live without her sight. When an experimental procedure allows her to see again, Darien is torn, knowing someone had to die in order for this to happen.

She embarks on a journey to personally thank the donor's family, but is too stunned to tell them the truth. Mixed emotions stir inside of her as she slowly gets to the know the people that feel like so much more than strangers to her. When the truth finally comes out, Darien walks away, taking the second chance that she's been given to go back to the only life she's ever known, but she's not the only one with a second chance at life.

Meant to Be by Graysen Morgen. Brandt is about to walk down the aisle with her girlfriend, when an unexpected chain of events turns her world upside down, causing her to question the last three years of her life. A chance encounter sparks a mix of rage and excitement that she has never felt before. Summer is living life and following her dreams, all the while, harboring a huge secret that could ruin her career. She believes that some things are better kept in the dark, until she has her third run-in with a woman she had hoped to never see again, and gives into temptation. Brandt and Summer start believing everything happens for a reason as they learn the true meaning of meant to be.

Coming Home by Graysen Morgen. After tragedy derails TJ Abernathy's life, she packs up her three year old son and heads back to Pennsylvania to live with her grandmother on the family farm. TJ picks back up where she left off eight years earlier, tending to the fruit and nut tree orchard, while learning her grandmother's secret trade. Soon, TJ's high school sweetheart and the same girl who broke her heart, comes back into her life, threatening to steal it away once again. As the weeks turn into months and tragedy strikes again, TJ realizes coming home was the best thing she could've ever done.

Special Assignment by Austen Thorne. Secret Service Agent Parker Meeks has her hands full when she gets her new assignment, protecting a Congressman's teenage daughter, who has had threats made on her life and been whisked away to a Christian boarding school under an alias to finish out her senior year. Parker is fine with the assignment, until she finds out she has to go undercover as a Canon Priest. The last thing Parker expects to find is a beautiful, art history teacher, who is intrigued by her in more ways than one.

Miracle at Christmas by Sydney Canyon. A Modern Twist on the Classic Scrooge Story. Dylan is a power-hungry lawyer who pushed away everything good in her life to become the best defense attorney in the, often winning the worst cases and keeping anyone with enough money out of jail. She's visited on Christmas Eve by her deceased law partner, who threatens her with a life in hell like his own, if she doesn't change her path. During the course of the night, she is taken on a journey through her past, present, and future with three very different spirits.

Bella Vita by Sydney Canyon. Brady is the First Officer of the crew on the Bella Vita, a luxury charter yacht in the Caribbean. She enjoys the laidback island lifestyle, and is accustomed to high profile guests, but when a U.S. Senator charters the yacht as a gift to his beautiful twin daughters who have just graduated from college and a few of their friends, she literally has her hands full.

Brides (Bridal Series book 2) by Graysen Morgen. Britton Prescott is dating the love of her life, Daphne Attwood, after a few tumultuous events that happened to unravel at her sister's wedding reception, seven months earlier. She's happy with the way things are, but immense pressure from her family and friends to take the next step, nearly sends her back to the single life. The idea of a long engagement and simple wedding are thrown out the window, as both families take over, rushing Britton and Daphne to the altar in a matter of weeks.

Cypress Lake by Graysen Morgen. The small town of Cypress Lake is rocked when one murder after another happens. Dani Ricketts, the Chief Deputy for the Cypress Lake Sheriff's Office, realizes the murders are linked. She's surprised when the girl that broke her heart in high school has not only returned home, but she's also Dani's only suspect. Kristen Malone has come back to Cypress Lake to put the past behind her so that she can move on with her life. Seeing Dani Ricketts again throws her off-guard, nearly derailing her plans to finally rid herself and her family of Cypress Lake.

Crashing Waves by Graysen Morgen. After a tragic accident, Pro Surfer, Rory Eden, spends her days hiding in the surf and snowboard manufacturing company that she built from the ground up, while living her life as a shell of the person that she once was. Rory's world is turned upside when a young surfer pursues her, asking for the one thing she can't do. Adler Troy and Dr. Cason Macauley from Graysen Morgen's bestselling novel: *Falling Snow*, make an appearance in this romantic adventure about life, love, and letting go.

Bridesmaid of Honor (Bridal Series book 1) by Graysen Morgen. Britton Prescott's best friend is getting married and she's the maid of honor. As if that isn't enough to deal with, Britton's sister announces she's getting married in the same month and her maid of honor is her best friend Daphne, the same woman who has tormented Britton for years. Britton has to suck it up and play nice, instead of scratching her eyes out, because she and Daphne are in both weddings. Everyone is counting on them to behave like adults.

Falling Snow by Graysen Morgen. Dr. Cason Macauley, a high-speed trauma surgeon from Denver meets Adler Troy, a professional snowboarder and sparks fly. The last thing Cason wants is a relationship and Adler doesn't realize what's right in front of her until it's gone, but will it be too late?

Fate vs. Destiny by Graysen Morgen. Logan Greer devotes her life to investigating plane crashes for the National Transportation Safety Board. Brooke McCabe is an investigator with the Federal Aviation Association who literally flies by the seat of her pants. When Logan gets tangled in head games with both women will she choose fate or destiny?

Just Me by Graysen Morgen. Wild child Ian Wiley has to grow up and take the reins of the hundred year old family business when tragedy strikes. Cassidy Harland is a little surprised that she came within an inch of picking up a gorgeous stranger in a bar and is shocked to find out that stranger is the new head of her company.

Love Loss Revenge by Graysen Morgen. Rian Casey is an FBI Agent working the biggest case of her career and madly in love with her girlfriend. Her world is turned upside when tragedy strikes. Heartbroken, she tries to rebuild her life. When she discovers the truth behind what really happened that awful night she decides justice isn't good enough, and vows revenge on everyone involved.

Natural Instinct by Graysen Morgen. Chandler Scott is a Marine Biologist who keeps her private life private. Corey Joslen is intrigued by Chandler from the moment she meets her. Chandler is forced to finally open her life up to Corey. It backfires in Corey's face and sends her running. Will either woman learn to trust her natural instinct?

Secluded Heart by Graysen Morgen. Chase Leery is an overworked cardiac surgeon with a group of best friends that have an opinion and a reason for everything. When she meets a new artist named Remy Sheridan at her best friend's art gallery she is captivated by the reclusive woman. When Chase finds out why Remy is so sheltered will she put her career on the line to help her or is it too difficult to love someone with a secluded heart?

In Love, at War by Graysen Morgen. Charley Hayes is in the Army Air Force and stationed at Ford Island in Pearl Harbor. She is the commanding officer of her own female-only service squadron and doing the one thing she loves most, repairing airplanes. Life is good for Charley, until the day she finds herself falling in love while fighting for her life as her country is thrown haphazardly into World War II. Can she survive being in love and at war?

Fast Pitch by Graysen Morgen. Graham Cahill is a senior in college and the catcher and captain of the softball team. Despite being an all-star pitcher, Bailey Michaels is young and arrogant. Graham and Bailey are forced to get to know each other off the field in order to learn to work together on the field. Will the extra time pay off or will it drive a nail through the team?

Submerged by Graysen Morgen. Assistant District Attorney Layne Carmichael had no idea that the sexy woman she took home from a local bar for a one night stand would turn out to be someone she would be prosecuting months later. Scooter is a Naval Officer on a submarine who changes women like she changes uniforms. When she is accused of a heinous crime she is shocked to see her latest conquest sitting across from her as the prosecuting attorney.

Vow of Solitude by Austen Thorne. Detective Jordan Denali is in a fight for her life against the ghosts from her past and a Serial Killer taunting her with his every move. She lives a life of solitude and plans to keep it that way. When Callie Marceau, a curious Medical Examiner, decides she wants in on the biggest case of her career, as well as, Jordan's life, Jordan is powerless to stop her.

Igniting Temptation by Sydney Canyon. Mackenzie Trotter is the Head of Pediatrics at the local hospital. Her life takes a rather unexpected turn when she meets a flirtatious, beautiful fire fighter. Both women soon discover it doesn't take much to ignite temptation.

One Night by Sydney Canyon. While on a business trip, Caylen Jarrett spends an amazing night with a beautiful stripper. Months later, she is shocked and confused when that same woman re-enters her life. The fact that this stranger could destroy her career doesn't bother her. C.J. is more terrified of the feelings this woman stirs in her. Could she have fallen in love in one night and not even known it?

Fine by Sydney Canyon. Collin Anderson hides behind a façade, pretending everything is fine. Her workaholic wife and best friend are both oblivious as she goes on an emotional journey, battling a potentially hereditary disease that her mother has been diagnosed with. The only person who knows what is really going on, is Collin's doctor. The same doctor, who is an acquaintance that she's always been attracted to, and who has a partner of her own.

Shadow's Eyes by Sydney Canyon. Tyler McCain is the owner of a large ranch that breeds and sells different types of horses. She isn't exactly thrilled when a Hollywood movie producer shows up wanting to film his latest movie on her property. Reegan Delsol is an up and coming actress who has everything going for her when she lands the lead role in a new film, but there one small problem that could blow the entire picture.

Light Reading: A Collection of Novellas by Sydney Canyon. Four of Sydney Canyon's novellas together in one book, including the bestsellers Shadow's Eyes and One Night.

Visit us at www.tri-pub.com